Into The Land of Snows

Ellis Nelson

The scanning, uploading and distribution of this book via the Internet or via any other means without the permission of the publisher is illegal and punishable by law. Please purchase only authorized editions and do not participate in or encourage the electronic piracy of copyrighted materials. Your support of the author's rights is appreciated.

This is a work of thought provoking fiction. Names, characters, places, and incidents are either the product of the author's imagination or are used fictitiously. Any resemblance to actual events, places, organizations, or persons, living or dead, is entirely coincidental. Though the message is real, and we hope it touches you the way it touched us.

INTO THE LAND OF SNOWS
BY ELLIS NELSON
ALL RIGHTS RESERVED
Copyright © 2012, ELLIS NELSON
ISBN# 978-1-938257-01-8
Cover Art ® 2012 by Winterheart Design
Edited by Sasha Vivelo

Electronic Publication Date: February 2012

Print Publication Date: February 2012

This book may not be reproduced or used in whole or in part by any means existing without written permission from the publisher, Jupiter Gardens Press, PO Box 191, Grimes, IA 50111

For more information to learn to more about this, or any other author's work, please visit http://www.jupitergardenspress.com/

Entertaining just a doubt
Tears to tatters worldly existence.
                    Aryadeva

REALITY AND ILLUSION

Chapter One

The phone rang at an ungodly hour. In the darkness, Blake reached across his desk and clicked it on.

"Hello?" he said, wiping the gunk from his eyes.

"Hi, Blake. It's Dad," came the response.

"Dad?"

"Listen, I got a call from your mother." The line crackled with static.

Blake threw his legs over the side of the bed and sat up. "Where are you?"

Mumble, mumble crack. "...at Base Camp. Look, I can't get away, so the best I can do is have you come here," Dad said.

"Come there? To Everest?" Blake said with disbelief. He dug his toe into the carpet and reminded himself he wasn't dreaming.

"Yes, here. Your mother is very upset."

"I know, but she'll calm down in a couple of days," Blake answered.

Dad's tone turned harsh. "You're coming here and we're going to straighten this out."

Blake drew in a cold breath and pleaded, "This is not a big deal. Everyone is overreacting. Besides, I can't come there. I'm in the middle of school. Maybe over the break. I know Mom will calm down. Look, this isn't necessary."

Static filled the line. "...not open to discussion. You are in big trouble and your butt is mine for the next few months. I've talked this all out with your mother and she'll help you get ready. I'll see you in a couple of weeks."

"But Dad—"

Click. The phone went dead. Blake let it drop into his lap. He climbed under the covers and pulled his comforter up close. With his back against the headboard, he shivered and wondered why everyone was making this out to be so important. On top of that, this was the first time he had heard from his father in the many months following the divorce, and the phone call hadn't been the warm reunion Blake sought. Why had Dad felt compelled to call in the middle of the night? Everyone was acting like this was a really serious thing, and it just wasn't. Go to Everest? That was crazy! He'd talk to Mom in the morning and once she truly heard what he had to say, she'd agree and Dad would back off his insane idea. Blake chuckled. Base Camp, Everest, yeah, right!

Chapter Two

"Don't worry. I'll get you to your father," the pilot said. He gave Blake a sharp rap on the back. Blake climbed on board the chopper, struggling with his gear. All his efforts to change his mother's mind about the trip had failed completely. He fell into the nearest seat and dropped his pack at his feet. Several men climbed in and buckled up next to him.

The helicopter rose and headed northeast, the chopper blades slicing through the frigid air. Blake McCormack settled into his seat, trying to make himself comfortable. More out of habit than anything else, he ran a hand through his wild, dark hair tipped with burgundy accents. He unzipped his jacket just enough to adjust the Egyptian ankh that scratched at his chest. A quick sideways glance at the man next to him made him wonder what these men might be thinking. Surely, a sixteen year old heading to Base Camp on Everest was unusual.

Three climbers with their own packs crammed in around Blake. Their excitement filled the small cabin even in the silence forced by the deafening noise of the helicopter. Blake pushed his fear down and puffed out his chest. He watched as a small Sherpa village vanished from the landscape behind him. Exiting the U-shaped, western-facing valley, the sacred mountain, Khumbila, rose in the north. Ahead lay the vast Himalayas.

Blake glanced out the window. "Wow!" he said, but no one heard him over the roar of the chopper.

As the mountains rose in the distance, Blake forced himself to think about his situation. Here he was, headed for the highest mountain in the world at the request of his father. Not a request, really. It had been a demand. Months had passed after the divorce and not a word had come from his father. And it was Dad who wanted the divorce, not Mom. All this was Dad's fault.

A gust pushed the helicopter sideways and Blake instantly snapped back to the present. He dug deep into the pockets of his down jacket and retrieved the two Diamox tablets given to him before takeoff. The medicine would act to minimize the effects of acute mountain sickness. That was what he'd been told, at least. One of the climbers across from him smiled and nodded as Blake threw the pills into his mouth and swallowed. Silently, he prayed they'd be effective.

How many times had he heard his father recount stories about climbers with altitude sickness? Dizziness, headaches, nausea, vomiting—he replayed the symptoms in his head, a technique that came to him naturally, as a doctor's son. Come on, Diamox, do your thing!

Already on the road ten days, Blake yawned with exhaustion from traveling. The journey had brought him from his home in Ohio to the foothills of the Himalayas with most of that time spent on planes. Landing in Katmandu had been a trip. Even the guidebooks hadn't prepared him for that. Talk about stepping back in time. A few days in the city and he was headed for Everest in a rugged SUV. It jarred and bounced Blake along for another couple of days until finally he faced the last leg of the arduous trip by helicopter. Anxious to get somewhere, he squeezed both gloved hands just to make sure he could still feel them. The higher the chopper rose, the more frigid the cabin became, and he shivered in spite of the blinding sunshine that poured through the windows.

"Look!" the largest of the climbers screamed. He thrust a hand toward a window. Blake only registered his meaning when the thickly padded finger thumped the glass.

Everyone turned to see what the man was pointing to. Blake craned his neck to look around the man next to him. On the ground, a dark shape sprang across a snow covered landscape only to disappear behind a rock face.

It was over before anyone could truly comprehend the event.

"What was that?" Blake screamed at the top of his lungs.

Two of the climbers shook their heads. The other shrugged and leaned in toward him. "Bear?" he shouted into Blake's ear.

Blake nodded.

Soon they were high enough to get a good look at the sprawling mountain range. One of the climbers pointed out a window. Blake gasped. Even in March, jagged snow-covered peaks sliced into the sky. Roughly hewn rocks stabbed through, making the mountains blue-gray. The valleys below held puffy cumulous clouds. Blake wondered when he'd see Mount Everest. A few minutes passed as everyone stared out the window, transported into a dream-like landscape of stark beauty.

They passed over two small villages where families tended potato plots amongst the barren terrain. Still ascending, they flew toward the Buddhist gompa of Tengboche. The stone monastery projected its presence over the whole valley while nestled in a high altitude forest.

One of the climbers poked at the window again. The others nodded and broke into broad grins. Blake knew their exhilaration meant they had spotted Everest. Excited and scared, Blake peered out into the bright day. He squinted against the blinding sunshine, and his jaw dropped. Far off and higher than he ever would have imagined, cotton candy puffs wrapped around the peak with the famous white fang hidden behind those clouds. In his mind's eye, he could see the summit.

Blake rummaged through his pack and retrieved his camera. He snapped a few quick shots, knowing they probably wouldn't be very good. But it would serve as his record of actually being there.

The force of the climbing helicopter pinned Blake in his seat. As the chopper rose, the engines strained. He balled his fists up and forced himself to take deep, rhythmic breaths. Relaxing, he told himself it would be okay. This would be the adventure of a lifetime, and he'd be able to tell people about the time he went to Everest. Even tough Slade, his best friend, would be impressed.

Instead of heading over the formidable mountains, the chopper cut west to follow a well-worn trekking trail. Two rivers crossed and separated, and in the valley a few scattered buildings sat amid a picture-postcard landscape. A long, dark line snaked its way from the village. Blake recognized this to be a yak train, but only because he had read about them.

The helicopter swept due north for its approach to Base Camp. More climbing, forever climbing. Blake wondered if they'd ever be high enough. The isolation and desolation as they grew closer to the peaks resonated in his soul. How could he be so thrilled and so scared at the same time?

Over rustic lodges and a blue glacier lined with ice seracs, Blake took in the harsh terrain. From photographs in books he knew that the climbers would face an even more hostile environment during their climb. The chopper descended suddenly, and around him the men started to pick up their packs.

The helicopter set down gently and the men unbuckled and hopped out. Last out, Blake managed to jump down just as the pilot killed the motor. No one was there to meet the chopper and he hesitated, uncertain what he should do. He had thought that his father would, at least, be there to greet him. But of course not. He had better things to do, just as always. Glancing over his shoulder, he saw the three climbers starting up a steep, rocky slope.

Throwing his pack over his shoulder, Blake ran after them. He fought the incline and finally called out.

"Hey, do any of you know Dr. McCormack?"

The smallest of the men turned around and said, "Sure. He's our team doc. He's at the camp just above us." Although the man was not as tall as the others, he was powerfully built. Close-cut blond hair and his direct approach gave him a military air.

The man's eyes narrowed and he asked, "Are you climbing?"

"No. I'm just going to see my dad," Blake responded. He suddenly felt very small amongst these rugged men.

"Ah, you're the doc's kid. Glad to hear that. You had me scared. I'm Nic, and this is Brian, and Jacques," he said, pointing to his companions.

Blake felt dwarfed standing next to Brian. The intimidating 6'4" frame towered over him. His curly, brown mass of hair that looked like it had never seen a comb softened the impact of Brian's physical size. He nodded and flashed a cock-eyed smile.

"Hi, I'm Blake."

"Bonjour," Jacques said. He extended his hand.

Blake shook hands as Jacques swiped a thick mane of long, blond hair from his eyes. Underneath, stylish European sunglasses hid much of his face.

"Well, Blake, let's get you to your dad," Nic said.

Chapter Three

"Please, Diamox," Blake quietly said to himself. His breathing became labored as he huffed and puffed his way towards camp.

"Come on, kid, we're almost there," Nic called over his shoulder. "Hey Brian, grab that pack from him. He's not used to this."

Brian stood waiting for Blake to catch up. When Blake neared him, he made a deliberately wide arc around Brian.

"No, thanks. I can do it," Blake said.

Uncomfortable with his last growth spurt, Blake hunched over under the weight of the pack. He tried to breathe deeply to get the oxygen he needed.

Base Camp came into sight as they crested a small knoll. Huddled in a vast valley and framed by a blue sky lay a cluster of buildings. The structures were crude. Lopsided stone huts covered with tarps sat on a gravel base. Modern tents in all sizes and shapes filled in around the permanent buildings. Strung from east to west over the small city, prayer flags fluttered in the wind. Their colors were the only thing that made the place cheery. Remnants of the last snow could still be seen weaving through the gorge and in the distance, Blake saw several people milling about the campsite. No one paid any attention to the newly arrived climbers.

Under a bright sun with just a hint of chill, Blake struggled to keep up, his breath came in fits and starts and already his muscles ached.

As they passed the first hut, Nic said to the group, "Let's find Noel and get the kid situated."

Blake scowled at being referred to as 'the kid', but what could he do about it?

Continuing through the encampment, they came to a circle of tents where two men sat in metal framed chairs, reading. The noise from the group trudging through disturbed them and one looked up. A wide, toothy smile greeted the visitors, and the man rose.

"Nic, Brian, and Frenchy! Welcome to the top of the world!" the man said, eyeing each of them in turn. Nic extended a hand, which was grasped and vigorously pumped.

"Not exactly, the top of the world, but pretty damn close. How's it going, Noel?" Nic answered.

Visibly older than the rest, Noel's bald head shone brilliantly through his comb-over of red hair. His intensely blue eyes and affable manner defined his presence.

"It's going all right. And who's this?" Noel said, looking toward Blake.

"That's Doc McCormack's kid."

"His name is Blake," Brian said as he stepped forward and shook hands with Noel.

"Well, the Doc's over in that hut across the way, but I know he's seeing one of those Italian guys. Saw him go in a few minutes ago," Noel said.

Noel kicked at the chair of the man still reading and continued, "Go tell the Doc that the rest of the guys are here and they brought his son up."

Noel commandeered a few more camping chairs, and the group sat among the tents. A sense of renewed camaraderie sparked as the climbers shared coffee and talked about the impending ascent. Blake held his coffee cup and sipped at the hot, bitter fluid, only half listening to the men. Where was his father? What was taking so long? He had come halfway around the world only to be left with strangers and be put off again. He pushed an index finger into the coffee and swirled it around. He

Into The Land of Snows | 11

inscribed B, L, A, K, E one letter at a time. Each letter made him angrier. He felt used. Or useless. So useless that his own father couldn't be bothered to get his ass out of a hut and over to him.

Blake's coffee had grown cold by the time Andrew McCormack left his clinic and made his way to the group of climbers. A tall, blond man with lanky limbs, Doc McCormack swaggered up. Blake had his height, but not his easygoing nature.

"Hey, guys! Glad you could make it," the doc said as he approached the gathering.

Startled by the familiar voice, Blake jumped and the coffee sloshed, drenching his black jeans. He jumped to his feet, embraced by his father.

"Blake!" Dad said enthusiastically.

Blake's arms stayed at his sides. He said nothing as he looked into his father's eyes. The anger did not diffuse.

"Sorry I couldn't come right away. I had a patient. So, how was the trip?" he said, dropping his arms and leading Blake back toward the clinic.

A patient again. Blake remembered all the other times patients had come first. He had always come in second. He came in second when he played soccer, when he played piano, when he had the lead in that play.... Second, always second. It would never change. Even in this remote environment where he thought things might be different, they wouldn't be. What a fool, he thought. Why did I think it would be different here?

His father opened the crooked clinic door and repeated himself. "How was the trip?"

Blake stepped through the doorway and grumbled, "All right, I guess."

The interior of the hut was more comfortable than Blake had expected. The walls were lined with brown paper insulation and the few windows allowed the high plateau sunshine to warm the interior. A small office sat partitioned off from the back area where Blake could just make out an examining table. Dad pulled out a chair and motioned for him to sit.

Blake fell into the chair and slid his pack to the floor. Grateful to sit, he relaxed and the altitude started to have its way with him. His head began to throb with a dull headache.

Dad hurried off to the examining area and soon returned.

"Here you go, hot chocolate with the mini marshmallows. It's got to be better than that mud Noel calls coffee. Remember when I'd take you over to the park sledding and then we'd have hot chocolate?" Dad said. He took a seat across the table from Blake.

"No."

"Really? Well, you were only three or four then. But I remember you wouldn't drink it unless it had mini marshmallows."

"I'm not four anymore."

"I can see that. Looks like you grew a foot since I last saw you." Dad sipped his chocolate and leaned forward. "What's with all the ear piercings?" he said as he playfully flicked Blake's left ear.

Blake recoiled but said nothing.

Dad returned to sipping and blowing on his hot chocolate. Blake saw him struggle with what to say next. While Dad figured out his approach, Blake crossed his arms over his chest and remembered how all this was Dad's fault anyway. It was his fault the divorce happened. It was his fault he had to move with Mom back to her hometown with her old friends. It was his fault he had to go to that new school and leave all his friends behind. His whole wreck of a life, Dad's fault.

"Look Blake, I know the divorce was tough on you. I know things haven't been easy."

Blake nodded. "Easy? Right. Try you ruined my whole freakin' life," he said quietly.

"I know. I know you feel that way. But eventually, things are going to settle down and your mother and I just want to keep you safe until things get better."

Blake looked at the floor. "Why do you think things are going to get better? You split, Mom falls apart, and I move to Podunk nowhere. You really don't have a clue about what's going on, do you?" Blake stared into his father's eyes.

Dad pushed back on his chair, lifting the front legs off the floor. "And your solution is to turn to drugs?" The question hung in the air as if a challenge.

"It's just a little marijuana and no, I'm not hooked."

"I hope not. You won't find it up here. Life's tough enough without those complications."

The static of the communications equipment erupted with voices. Dad jumped up and took hold of the receiver. Blake couldn't make out anything being said over the static.

"Roger that. Have him come by the clinic," Dad replied. He replaced the receiver and sat back down.

"Blake, life at Base Camp is pretty hard. Maybe not hard, more like basic. There's lots of quiet time punctuated with manic activity. You're here because I'm here. It was too late to cancel this job. So, we're going to try to make the best of it. This is an opportunity to be around some amazing people. Guys you'd never meet anywhere else. You're going to have to be flexible. Do what I ask. The work won't be hard and hopefully we'll have an easy season."

Blake stared back. He couldn't believe it. Dad wasn't even going to apologize for not being there for him after the divorce. He wasn't even going to try to explain his absence. *Why should he? He doesn't care about what I'm going through. He never has. As long as he gets to do what he wants, everything's great.*

Finally, Blake nodded reluctantly and took his first gulp of chocolate.

Dad went to the door and stepped partially outside. He cupped his hands and called out, "Noel! Hey, Noel!"

Within a minute or two, Noel appeared at the door, talking with Dad in hushed tones. Together, they approached.

"Blake, I want you to go with Noel. He's going to take you by my hut to drop your stuff off and then over to the mess hall. I'd take you, but I've got a Sherpa coming in with frostbite. I'll catch up with you later."

Chapter Four

Blake followed Noel and they weaved a circuitous route through the makeshift small town.

"Man, you sure are lucky, Blake. I would have killed to come to Base Camp when I was your age. I bet the doc is going to end up with a climber in the family yet," Noel said as they walked across the camp.

Blake gulped at the thought of ever doing any climbing and quickly tried to change the subject. "I never thought Base Camp would be this big."

Noel chuckled. "Yeah. A lot of people are surprised. Already, there are over three hundred people here representing almost a dozen different nations."

Blake scanned the area. For men about to climb the tallest mountain in the world, their lack of activity surprised him. Small groups were gathered here or there talking or laughing. Others were alone reading or listening to music on headsets.

"When do you climb?" Blake asked.

"That's a good question. This early in the season the weather's still pretty rough. We have to wait for an opening. And then the rest of the guys just showed up today and they have to acclimatize."

"How long does that take?" Blake asked. He wondered how long it would take him to adjust.

They passed a Sherpa piling rocks to rebuild the side of one of the huts that had collapsed.

"It depends on the climber. The guidelines say it takes about ten weeks, but some of the guys speed up the process by going to the Alps first. Right now, we're all trying to 'climb high and sleep low'. You know that one, don't you?"

Blake kicked a rock off the path. "Yeah. I've read about it. You climb during the day but come back down to a lower camp to sleep. Then you move up the mountain, each time sleeping at higher camps. It helps you to acclimatize faster."

"Right. So a bunch of us went out this morning, but by late afternoon everyone will be back at camp. Meanwhile, the Sherpa teams are working on the route. Each season they replace any equipment that's old or falling apart. They help us climb safely."

Arriving at a small hut, Noel said, "This is it. I'll give you an hour or so to settle in and then I'll be back for you. You hungry?"

"Not really."

Noel laughed. "You will be by the time I get back."

Alone, Blake dropped his pack near one of two cots and sat down. He felt winded and a little lightheaded. The place had no windows, and even at midday, it was dark.

Nearby, a small crate supported a torch. Blake reached for it and snapped it on. Stashed under one of the cots, were food, clothing, extra shoes, and equipment. He recognized a couple of his school textbooks that Mom had air mailed from back home. In the open spaces along the wall, crates stood piled to the ceiling. A small stove sat alone at the far end of the room. Blake sighed as he realized that life would be far from comfortable. Basic had been the word Dad had used. He forced himself to take a few deep breaths then he unpacked his backpack, placing everything under the free cot.

To ease the boredom, Blake had brought his MP3 player and solar recharger. A couple of books including works by Edgar Allen Poe and Dante rested beneath the bed. He sat back and popped his headset on. Music by Siouxsie and the Banshees filled the empty space. He closed his eyes and withdrew into his music.

About an hour later, Noel banged and the door swung open. Blake removed the headset and put it aside. As they were leaving, Noel said, "Don't forget to turn off the light. We don't waste anything up here."

Blake extinguished the torch obediently and grabbed his digital camera. Noel led him toward the mess tent. The sun beat down intensely, contrasting sharply with the dark hut. Blake's eyes watered and he shoved his sunglasses on. Zigzagging their way through camp reminded Blake of a maze. He realized that Base Camp could be turned into its own version of Dungeons and Dragons and he chuckled at the thought of it. Maybe Slade would be interested in trying to create their own game when he returned home.

A final turn near the German encampment brought them to the shared mess tent. Looking behind him, Blake doubted he'd be able to retrace Noel's path back to the hut. Noel held the tent flap back for him and waited for him to step through.

The tent was wide open on the other side with half the space bathed in yellow light.

Six metal camp tables stood surrounded by aluminum framed chairs. At the far end sat a lone man sipping from a ceramic mug. He looked up, nodded, and smiled as Noel and Blake entered.

Even dressed in modern clothing, Blake recognized the man to be a Sherpa by his dark coloring and black hair that danced playfully in the breeze. His eyes were slits under strong arched eyebrows that perfectly counterbalanced his broad smile.

Blake paused and allowed Noel to step ahead of him.

"How's it going, Ang?" Noel called out.

The Sherpa rose as they approached, and Blake saw that the man was quite small.

"Ang, this is Blake McCormack, the doc's boy."

"I am happy to meet you," Ang said, bowing his head slightly.

"Good to meet you, too," Blake answered trying to sound as polite as possible.

Thumping Ang on the back, Noel said, "Ang is one of the most experienced guys on this season's team! He can tell you stories about climbs from now till next Tuesday and still not share his best ones. Take a seat, Blake."

Blake sat across from the Sherpa, who continued to smile.

"I'm going next door. What's on the menu, Ang?" Noel asked.

"Something they call beef stew."

"Right. Had it a couple of days ago, it wasn't bad. I'll get you some, Blake. Be right back."

Alone with the Sherpa, Blake couldn't think of anything to say. He circled his head to relieve his tight neck muscles until Brian and Jacques entered the room, breaking the uncomfortable silence. Each carried a plate and a mug, shuffling slowly as if each step was difficult. They came up behind Ang and paused. The aroma of spicy stew filled the space.

"May we join you? Ang, we must continue to practice your French," Jacques said.

Ang nodded. The two men sat down and began to eat.

After a few mouthfuls, Brian said, "This is pretty good, but I'm still missing the Tamel cafes. I know I'm not going to get banana fritters up here."

Jacques shook his head. "I do not miss Katmandu. The noise, the dirt, the stench. I am happy to be here away from that insanity." He continued to eat, but far more slowly than Brian. "Blake, did you get sick in Katmandu like I did? The food gave me a fever, vomiting, and diarrhea."

"No, I stayed with one of my dad's friends and never ate out. The food was weird though, too spicy for me."

Noel came back and set a plate of stew and a mug in front of Blake. "Eat up. Food here at Base Camp is the best you'll ever get on the mountain." All the men nodded. Noel turned and left. Blake saw him talking to two Sherpas who waited outside.

Blake took his first bite as Jacques laid his fork down and said, "I think the altitude is getting to me already. Ang, do you have any advice for this poor Frenchman?"

Ang took a sip from his mug and considered his response. "You should have walked into camp. Now it is too late. Your body will fight you. Then you will adjust. If it gets worse, go see the doctor."

Brian held his steaming mug with both hands, "Blake, how are you feeling? Do you know about altitude sickness?"

Blake's fork hung in the air as he answered. "I'm okay, so far. Back at the hut, I felt dizzy and nauseous, but eating helps. I know a little about altitude sickness. The higher you go, the less oxygen there is—so your body has to work harder to get it. Eventually, your marrow produces more red blood cells and that relieves some of the stress. Until you become acclimatized, you can have lots of symptoms. Everyone handles it differently." He smiled.

"Right. That's why you and I are doing better than Jacques. Everyone knows that Americans are tough and the French, well, what can I say...?" Brian gave Jacques a friendly shove while Jacques responded by rolling his eyes, unfit to fight back.

Noel left the Sherpas and returned to Blake. "I've got a few things to take care of. If you feel up to it, you can explore the camp. It's safe as long as you don't wander off."

Blake finished eating and Ang pulled out a stack of Polaroids from his pocket. He spread the images across the table. In each photo, a smiling Sherpa stared back at them.

"This is the team. We will have a contest. I will tell you each name today and tomorrow whoever can name the most will win a prize," Ang said.

"What's the prize?" Brian asked with excitement. "Money, booze, women? Can you get women up here?"

Jacques sighed, and Blake decided this would be a good time to look around the campsite.

Chapter Five

Blake stepped out into the full sun. The intense Himalayan light bounced off old snow and ice, hurting his eyes. He grabbed for his sunglasses. Noel emerged right behind him.

"Now remember, Blake, stay close. If you need anything, just ask," Noel said.

Blake put the sunglasses on. "Okay. I will," he said.

Noel nodded, called to a group of climbers, and hurried off to meet them. Blake walked alone through the camp. A gentle breeze wafted through the colorful prayer flags as he walked under them. Traversing rough terrain, Blake realized a glacier had deposited the rocky refuge at his feet. Well-worn pathways wove their way around clusters of tents.

Positioning himself to get a good picture of a valley, Blake snapped a few photos. The gentle brown slopes soon gave rise to mighty gray and white mountains. One set behind another, they grew larger in the distance. Something about the desolation and quiet sent a shiver down Blake's back. It was an odd sensation for a bright, sunny day. Deliberately, he spun around, shaking off the uneasiness he felt. He clicked a few more photos and moved on. His breathing became labored due to the altitude and he became aware of how much work it took to put one foot in front of the other.

Making his way through the camp, he thought about how it resembled an ant's nest. One trail would lead into another, heading for some place important. Another wove its way in an opposite direction and then suddenly it would end, abandoned. Blake pictured the men around him as ants. They were involved in purposeful activities that he didn't always understand or recognize.

At the intersection of two paths, Blake hopped to the side to allow two Sherpas to pass. They ran, carrying three aluminum ladders, smiling and chanting under their breath, "Om mani padme hum." Their physical strength and endurance made Blake only too aware of his own shortcomings. He struggled just to walk and yet the Sherpas showed no effects of oxygen deprivation.

Blake shook his head as he stepped back onto the trail. Click, click. He snapped photos of the Sherpas as they ran under a string of prayer flags. Blake recalled from climbing books that many Westerners found the incessant hum of the Sherpas' chanting somewhat unsettling, but for him it had the opposite effect. The mantras calmed him and provided the perfect anchoring mechanism to the towering mountains.

Turning a corner, he passed a group of Sherpas working with climbing rope and wondered if any of them were as tough as the legendary Sherpa climbers called the Tigers of the Snow. He had read about them while he was in the San Francisco airport waiting for a connection. Would any of these Sherpas go as high as those men this season?

He yawned and felt exhaustion wash over his body. Having seen a good portion of Base Camp, Blake felt more confident about his ability to get around alone. He easily retraced his steps, passing the mess tent and going on toward his new accommodations.

He settled into his cot. Even in the middle of the day with the intense light of the high altitude sun, Blake slept soundly.

Persistent rapping yanked him out of his dream. Disoriented, he sat up and shook himself awake. His body felt heavy and he fought to throw his legs off the bed.

"Who is it?"

Ang had poked his head into the hut looking for Blake. "Excuse me. I thought you might like to come to the ceremony."

Blake placed his feet on the floor and forced himself to stand. Every movement on the mountain required his full attention, and his mind was not working at full capacity. He finally managed to say, "What ceremony?"

"May I come in?" Ang answered.

"Sure." Blake stumbled a few steps forward and breathed deeply.

Ang continued, "The ceremony is known as puja. It blesses the climb. Everyone will be there."

Running a hand through his untamed hair, Blake responded, "Okay, sure, let's go."

Ang smiled, showing a lot of teeth, as he hurried Blake out of the room. Barely five feet tall, Ang Sherpa sped along the trail. Blake picked up his pace but soon realized his body was in rebellion. Several yards ahead, Ang stopped and waited. "I have forgotten that you are not used to her yet."

Blake let the comment pass, but Ang persisted. "You call her Everest. We call her Chomolungma, Goddess Mother of the World. We must ask permission of the gods before we climb."

Blake nodded. He wondered what his friend Slade would think of all of this.

The wind picked up and the sun receded, dropping the temperature from the midday's high. Blake felt the air's iciness sting his nostrils. Ang led him outside the camp. Not far away stood a stone monument. In its middle, a ten-foot pole supported lines of prayer flags that radiated from the chorten. Gathered at its base were the members of the expedition. Blake recognized Noel, Brian, and Jacques. Where was Dad? With another patient?

Ang took Blake to the men, who were laughing and joking together. Blake took a position near them but didn't join their conversation. Ang, still smiling, nodded to several other men who approached the group.

Blake surveyed the scene. Almost as tall as the giant Brian, the rectangular stone cairn reached into the sky and was made more impressive by the hanging yellow, green, red, white, and blue flags whipping in the strong wind. A small, dark man wearing the garb of a monk moved into position before the monument. His round face supported strong features. An intense orange shirt floated on top of his deep burgundy tunic. From his waist hung a small, silver key. With his head clean shaven, he exuded a deep calm. He quietly muttered to himself. Blake assumed the monk was chanting mantras, providing the Himalayas with its own unique music and magic.

The assembled group grew quiet and edged in toward the monk. Blake took a few steps away from Ang to get a better view of the ceremony. Behind the placid monk, incense rose in gentle, gray rivulets. Once above the crowd, the wind caught the incense trail and carried it off. Blake sniffed at the air to see if he could detect its scent. He couldn't. Apparently, only Chomolungma would be able to smell it.

Three Sherpa men separated themselves from the crowd, taking up positions near the monk. Each held a large, oblong book covered in brown leather. Together, they opened their books. As the monk bowed solemnly, the three men began to recite. The words were strange to Blake, but he assumed they must be words in the Sherpas' language. The sounds, melodic and repetitive, reminded him of poetry and yet there was a difference. As he looked at the group, Blake saw that the other Sherpas were moving their bodies to the gentle beat of the prayers. The sounds seemed to resound with everyone. The ceremony was not a social occasion or just a vestige of tradition, Blake noted. It had real meaning to these people.

Subconsciously, Blake began to sway with the crowd. The men turned page after page and still the crowd remained immersed. Suddenly, a hand placed on Blake's shoulder ripped him from his trance. He spun around to find his father standing behind him.

Blake whispered, "Late, as usual."

Apparently Dad didn't hear the comment. He smiled and stepped forward so that father and son stood side by side. Blake tried to concentrate on the ceremony again but found it impossible. His father's arrival killed the spell of solemn ambience and Blake felt anger rise in him.

The Sherpas finished reading and returned to the crowd. At the foot of the monument lay food and climbing gear for the expedition. Ice axes crisscrossed each other, looking like bizarre metal fencing. Crampons, metal spikes for boots, leaned precariously against the chorten. Nearby lay more ropes and supplies, all blessed by the ceremony.

A small satchel was passed around, and from it everyone scooped up a small handful of rice. Blake felt the weight of the rice in his hand and moved it to his face. He inhaled the nutty fragrance of brown rice. The wind lifted several grains from his hand and whisked them away. Quickly, he clasped his hand shut, saving the rest. The monk recited another prayer and everyone threw the rice into the air. Caught unaware, Blake hurried to hurl his rice into the winds of Everest. Smiles broke across the faces of the Sherpas as everyone shuffled to form rows in front of the monk.

From behind him, the monk picked up a set of red bands. He chanted, "Om mani padme hum," as he placed a band around each man's neck. Each then bowed, accepting the lama's blessing.

Blake bowed just like the others. The lama placed the band around him but did not move on to the next man. *Why doesn't he move on? What does he want? This is not good.* After an inordinate amount of time staring at his shoes, Blake finally raised his head. The holy man's eyes met his. Friendly, patient brown eyes focused on him.

His nervousness evaporated as he realized the lama wanted nothing. The monk bowed his head and moved on.

When the ceremony concluded, the crowd moved off and Blake was left standing near his father and Ang.

"It was a good puja, nothing went wrong. We will climb in the safety of the gods," Ang said.

Dad clapped a gloved hand on Blake's shoulder and shook him in agreement. "Yes! I'm sure of it."

Blake didn't respond out loud. Taking a few steps toward Ang proved to be enough to shirk off his father's touch. "When does the climbing start?" Blake asked Ang.

"Before dawn, Sherpas will leave camp and begin work on the trail. Many weeks will pass before climbers will try to summit."

Standing this close to Ang made Blake feel awkward. A recent growth spurt gave him height that made his new body seem strange to him. At this altitude with his body in open rebellion, Blake struggled to find himself within his own physical form.

The three headed back toward the camp. Passing a group of tents, Ang called out, "Dawa! Dawa, come!"

A tall, young Sherpa hustled to Ang's side. Blake recognized him as being one of the Sherpas carrying the ladders.

"Dawa. This is Blake, Doctor McCormack's son. Perhaps he can play checkers."

Dawa nodded with excitement and then seemed to remember himself as he thrust a hand forward to meet Blake. The two shook hands.

Doctor McCormack slapped Blake on the back, "Of course he can play checkers! He used to be really good at it. We used to play all the time."

Blake rolled his eyes.

Chapter Six

The last rays of the late afternoon sun fell on Base Camp as Dawa walked with Blake back toward the hut.

"You and I will play checkers soon?" Dawa asked.

Blake threw the door to the hut open. He yawned. "Yeah, sure—but not now. I'm exhausted."

Dawa bowed slightly at this and Blake disappeared inside.

Despite the nap he had managed to get that afternoon, he still felt tired and lightheaded. Blake sought the refuge of his bunk, completely worn out by the day's events. Not even the wafting scent of spaghetti sauce from the mess tent could dissuade him.

Sometime during the night he heard his father come in, but sleep pulled him under again. In his dream, he was a climber, part of a team. Near the summit of Everest, with Nic in the lead, the team pushed toward the top. Jacques came next singing "Frère Jacques." The men cleared the famous third step and it was Blake's turn. The step looked steep, and he had never done any real climbing before. Behind him, Brian started to give instructions, and Blake began to feel he could do it. Then Dad materialized behind Brian. Hands on hips, he shouted, "Get down right now!"

A horrifying sound of tearing ripped Blake from his dream. He sat bolt upright, shaking. The deafening noise continued and morphed into a high-pitched vibration. *What the hell?*

"Dad!"

The crash sounded like trains colliding. *Crashes on a mountain? Not possible. Earthquake?*

"It's all right, Blake. It's just the ice field. The seracs melt during the day. Sometimes they fall down," his father answered, sounding tired. "Go back to sleep."

Satisfied to have an answer, Blake pushed himself down into the blankets. The answer did not, however, soothe his nerves. He lay awake, staring at the ceiling and listening to the shifting and rumblings in the Khumbu Icefall.

He awoke several hours later to find the hut bathed in a warm, yellow glow. Glancing over at his father's bunk, he saw it was freshly made with Dad nowhere in sight. Blake yawned and stretched and considered whether or not he should just stay in bed. He shook off that notion when he remembered that some of the Sherpas would start work on the mountain that morning. He grabbed his travel kit and stumbled out to the latrine facilities.

Shortly after, he headed for the mess tent for a quick breakfast. Dawa stood at the front eating a biscuit, butter running down his chin.

"Hi," Blake said as he passed him.

"Good morning," Dawa answered, his Sherpa accent very apparent. "Today, we play the checkers?"

"Sure. Later, though. I have to eat."

Inside, Noel and Brian sat hunched over plates of eggs and bacon. Noel nodded and Brian waved. Blake fetched himself the same breakfast and eagerly joined them.

"Have they started yet? Has the team left?" Blake asked.

Brian stuffed his mouth full of eggs and responded anyway, "Yeah, they're on the mountain. Well, actually they're in the icefall."

"Had a pretty good crash last night. Did you hear it?" Noel said as he swallowed a gulp of coffee.

"It woke me up, but Dad said it was routine because of the melting," Blake responded.

"Yes, routine." Noel answered, nodding.

As the men finished eating, Brian reached into his jacket pocket and placed the Sherpa Polaroids on the table. In unison they called out each name until one face stumped them.

Noel slid the photo in front of Blake.

"That's Dawa."

Noel and Brian seemed impressed that he already knew the Sherpas. Really, he didn't know anyone beyond Ang and Dawa, but he didn't have to tell them that. He sat and finished his milk, reveling in the new respect the men had for him. Realizing that it was only a matter of time before another Sherpa photo was put in front of him, Blake decided to leave and maintain his reputation with the men.

"See you later," Blake said, smirking.

The Himalayan sun crept higher, bringing its welcome warmth. Prayer flags hung straight down and without any wind, the day was glorious. Blake headed toward the chorten. The sound of feet behind him made him reel around. Dawa caught up to him.

"I thought you might go up today," Blake said as he pointed toward the Khumbu Valley.

"No. I helped get the gear ready. Today I stay in camp. Boring."

"I'm going to the monument to see if the stuff's still there. Do you want to come?

"Yes."

Blake felt his energy return and he felt steadier on his legs. Not that he felt a hundred percent yet. He knew that might take a while. Still, Dawa and he walked together stride for stride.

When they reached the site of the previous night's puja, Blake saw that all the food and tools had been removed. Two streamers of prayer flags snaked around the foot of the chorten.

Freed by the wind from the top of the pole, the flags had dropped during the night. Dawa stopped short of the monument, shaking his head.

"Bad," he muttered more to himself than anyone else. Then Blake heard him start chanting a prayer.

He couldn't understand why Dawa would make a few decorations falling down such a big deal. The ceremony had gone smoothly. What did it matter that the next day a couple of flags were down?

Dawa continued to chant. His whole demeanor had taken on a stricken urgency.

"Look, we can retie the thing," Blake offered. "The monument isn't that big. We scramble up and one of us shimmies up the pole."

Dawa ceased chanting prayers, but still looked doubtful. He stepped up to the chorten and finding a toehold, started to climb. Hand over hand, he scaled the wall.

"Wait! You need the flags," Blake called. He gathered up the lines so that Dawa could reattach them.

Dawa reached the top of the monument and stood shaking the pole. Blake wrapped the rope around his fist and began climbing. Not as fast as Dawa, he found he sometimes had to kick several times and feel his way around. Finally, his foot would catch and support him moving up. On the top of the chorten, he found Dawa kneeling, ready to help him up.

Dawa scurried up the pole clutching the lines of flags and securely refastened them. He slid down as if he had done it countless times. Soon the two were on solid ground looking up, examining their work.

"The gods will be happy now," Dawa said.

"Now, we can play the checkers," Blake said, trying to imitate Dawa's Sherpa way of speaking.

Blake waited outside his father's hut for Dawa to bring his checkers set. He pulled two chairs around a makeshift table made from an ancient looking barrel and plopped down. Quickly bored, he sprang back into the cabin and grabbed his books. Flipping through *The Collected Works of Edgar Allen Poe*, he read through Lenora before Dawa appeared, carefully carrying a game box.

Dawa set the box down. "Do you prefer red or black?"

Blake considered the choice. Both colors appealed to his new Goth identity. He knew Slade would always have taken the black, but black was so safe, so predictable. Red meant excitement, passion, blood.

"Red."

Dawa could not restrain his feelings for the game. The respect he showed setting up the pieces was soon replaced by his fierce, competitive nature. Blake noticed how Dawa studied every move and took long moments to consider all his options. The game absorbed his complete attention. It reminded Blake of elementary school when everyone played games with intense seriousness. There had even been friendships lost over the bad feelings that had never healed. He remembered the time Troy decked Matt when he lost at Monopoly. Troy's Dad pulled him off and sent him to time out while he apologized to Matt. That had been a heck of a sleepover.

Although a bit rusty, Blake gave Dawa a spirited game of checkers. In the end, three black kings chased two red kings around the board. The game grew tiresome and Blake artfully sacrificed one and then the other king. Dawa's intense concentration broke with the thrill of victory.

"Thank you for playing. I am sure you will win next time," Dawa said, shifting the focus away from himself.

"Yeah, good game!"

Dawa dutifully packed up the game as Blake reached for his book. While most of the books he brought to camp had been suggested by Slade, he had a couple of small travel guides filled with pictures. As Dawa sat across from him smiling, Blake reached down and retrieved the guidebook for India and handed it to him.

Absorbed in the travel book, Dawa didn't seem to notice when Blake slipped back into the hut to retrieve his camera. The first click startled Dawa from the book, but he quickly smiled for Blake. A few more shots and both boys returned to their books.

Later, as Blake finished his book, he saw Dawa flip back to the beginning of the travel guide.

"Have you ever been to India?" Blake asked.

"No. I have been to Katmandu, but the Indian cities are much bigger. One day I will go there and see these things," Dawa said. He closed the book and flashed a smile as he tried to hand the book back to Blake.

"No, you keep it. That way you'll know exactly what you want to see when you get there."

Clearly touched, Dawa jumped up and bowed slightly. With much formality and emotion he managed to say, "Thank you, Blake. I appreciate your gift. I will take good care of it indeed."

Blake had given lots of gifts to friends and family. Usually the person receiving the gift would say thanks and he would answer with the usual 'you're welcome' or 'sure, no problem.' But Blake had never seen anyone who seemed as truly grateful and honored as Dawa was. It was such a little thing, and yet it had made a big impression. He tried to rise to the occasion by saying, "I'm glad you like it and hope you will find it useful."

Dawa nodded and left, clutching his treasure.

Chapter Seven

Blake sprawled orangutan-like between two camp chairs, listening to his MP3 player. The strain of several hours of playing finally drained the machine. He opened his eyes and dragged the headset from his ears. The sun had moved west and the growl of his stomach let him know it was well after lunchtime. He rose stiffly from his chair and set out for the mess tent.

Not far from the tent he came upon Brian working on some gear.

"How's it going?" Brian called as Blake approached.

"All right I guess. I'm headed to the tent for lunch. How was it?"

Brian flashed a smile, "I've had better. But it'll do."

Blake laughed and continued on. A pair of geese honked as they flew past overhead.

He craned his neck to get a better look and marveled that even at Base Camp, wildlife persisted. He shook his head as he watched the dark-headed geese gain altitude, heading for Everest.

The Sherpa cook stood alone peeling potatoes when Blake entered. The man put the knife down and silently ladled out a bowl of soup. Blake noticed a silver and turquoise amulet hanging from the cook's neck. It seemed out of place on top of the rich, red flannel shirt the Sherpa wore. Blake drew in the fragrant aroma of the chicken broth as the cook placed a biscuit on top.

A few hearty spoonfuls of soup soon soothed his growling stomach. Blake felt awkward sitting alone in the mess tent. He broke the biscuit in half and stuffed it into his mouth. That was a mistake. The dry biscuit lodged in his throat and Blake gasped for breath. He grabbed his water glass and tried to force down a gulp. The water trickled out over his chin and then ran full force down the front of his shirt. Unable to make a sound, Blake panicked and jumped to his feet just as Ang walked into the tent.

Ang smiled to see Blake, but didn't seem to recognize the urgency of the situation. Blake grabbed his neck with both hands and then pointed frantically to the biscuit. Ang rushed to Blake and got behind him. Blake felt two powerful arms wrap around his chest as he began to sink to the floor. Two quick abdominal thrusts propelled the biscuit out of his windpipe and across the room. Blake crumpled in Ang's arms, gasping for breath. Ang lowered Blake to the floor to recover.

A few moments later Ang said, "Bread is dry from altitude. It can kill like the mountain." He cocked a strange, half smile.

Blake forced down air and saliva. Was Ang trying to be funny? "Thanks, I'll remember that." Blake picked himself off the floor. "I'm glad you came in. I don't know what I would have done by myself. Thanks." Self-consciously, he headed back to his seat. Blake would have liked to have said more, but he realized this was Everest. Guys risk their lives every day. Choking to death on a biscuit, while scary, wasn't exactly macho. He could almost hear Slade chuckle over the incident. "Blake, my man, you go to the freakin' top of the world and give it up to a biscuit. That's not even half funny." And he'd be right.

Ang patted Blake on the shoulder and shuffled off toward the kitchen. Blake could hear the cook and Ang converse in another language. Sharp guffaws erupted from the next room and Blake wondered if they were laughing at him. Would Ang tell everyone at camp how he had rescued him from some bad bread? How long would it be before Dad and the others knew?

Blake pushed small bits of biscuit and copious amounts of broth into his mouth, chewed and swallowed. He'd stop it before it went any further. Blake forced his way into the kitchen, pushing between the men to place his dirty dishes near a wash tub. He glared at Ang as he slammed the dishes down. He turned on his heels and left feeling satisfied.

Outside, a crisp breeze lifted the prayer flags. Blake zipped his parka and stormed toward the medical hut. He could at least head off some embarrassment by telling Dad how it happened. By downplaying the whole incident he would avoid looking like a wimp and Ang wouldn't be much of a hero.

So involved in developing the proper spin to his story, he didn't see Dawa until they nearly collided.

"Hello, Blake, I have something for you," Dawa said. He extended both hands.

Blake took the object and realized it was an old-fashioned camera. The small, black box easily fit in his palm, but it weighed more than modern cameras.

"What's this for?" Blake asked.

"I found it last spring when I first came to work here. You like to take pictures. Now you can take more pictures. It is yours." Dawa grinned.

But what on earth was he going to do with an antique camera? He already had the compact digital camera Mom gave him last Christmas. Dawa smiled with such pride that the gesture slapped Blake in the face. Dawa had presented him with a gift, just as he had given Dawa the gift of the travel book.

Raising the camera to his eye, "Thanks. I'm sure I'll get lots of great shots with this," Blake answered, exuberantly. He hoped Dawa wouldn't notice his overacting.

"You are welcome." Dawa beamed ear to ear.

"What's that?" Dad said as Blake entered the medical building. Seated at his desk, Dad scribbled notes as he went through a pile of papers.

"Just something Dawa gave me." Blake stowed the camera on a shelf next to some gauze bandages. He considered telling Dad about the biscuit incident, but he decided it could wait.

Dad grabbed another pile of papers and rose from his work. "I have some inventory lists you can help me with. I've unpacked everything, and now it's time to make sure it's all here. Basically, I need you to count items and mark down anything that's missing."

Blake didn't answer right away. It was a form of protest, but in the end he knew he would have to comply. Besides, there wasn't much else to do unless he challenged Dawa to another round of checkers or investigated the possibility of women at camp for Brian.

Reluctantly he said, "Sure."

Dad handed him a thick document that read 'Medical Supplies Inventory.' As Blake leafed through it, he realized that it would take hours to count the hundreds of items listed.

"What if I don't know what something is?" Blake asked.

Dad stood by the radio listening to the static cackle coming over the airwaves. "Just ask." He fiddled with buttons and turned the sound up.

"This is going to take a while. Can I go get my MP3 player?"

"Sure," Dad answered waving him off.

As he strolled across camp, Blake considered his options in music. His MP3 player allowed him to have access to hundreds of selections. He had downloaded lots of songs currently on the radio but his personal favorites were from Goth bands. There was Bauhaus, Siouxsie and the Banshees, Sisters of Mercy, and Dead Can Dance. Slade had even recommended some new stuff, so he wouldn't be out of touch when he got back home. He decided to listen to the classics because Slade would expect a

Into The Land of Snows | 37

full report and he didn't feel inventorying would allow him to concentrate effectively enough on the new music.

Blake grabbed his MP3 player. He stepped out of the hut and into mayhem. Men yelled and rushed about. Sherpas grabbed up equipment, heading for the center of camp. All the activity took on an air of urgency, bordering on panic, and Blake knew instantly something bad had happened. He ran toward the medical hut, fighting his body every step of the way. *Dad will know what's going on.*

He ran past a group of Sherpas that included Dawa and Ang. The group chattered nervously in their own tongue. Blake pushed on and finally burst through the hut's door.

The sound blasting from the radio almost knocked him over. Dad frantically threw open cabinets and cast supplies into open medical kits on the floor. Brian wrestled heavy metallic boxes out past him. Noel stacked gurneys near the door, and Blake felt his knees sag.

Chapter Eight

"What's going on?" Blake shouted trying to be heard over the radio.

Dad either didn't hear him or else he was purposely ignoring him.

Jerking his head up as he stuck the gurneys under his arm, Noel shouted, "Avalanche!"

Blake held the door open as Noel came through. Outside he followed, trying to absorb what was happening. Sherpas relieved Brian and Noel of the medical gear and hurried toward the icefall. Throughout camp Blake noticed that the Sherpas all seemed to be doing something, but the Western climbers stood around in staggered groups looking helpless. Three men, donning hats with small German flags, set off behind the Sherpas.

"Is it a rescue?" Blake asked.

"Of sorts. Ten Sherpas and two German climbers were up there when it happened. A snow wall smashed into the icefall where the Sherpas were securing lines. Eight Sherpas are accounted for. Some hurt. That's all we know right now." Noel's tone was grave.

Blake returned to his father who stood with his hand on his forehead, deep in thought. He brought the hand down and glanced at Blake and then charged out of the room. Blake couldn't think of a thing to say to him and he knew enough to stay out of the way.

Pushing the door open a crack, Blake saw his father talking to Ang. Ang's ever-present smile was gone. He nodded once in a while as his hands took refuge in his pockets, his eyes avoiding contact. Ang straightened and looked at Dad. He said something and then the two men shook hands and Ang walked off.

Blake pulled the door closed and fell into a chair, waiting. Moments later, Dad came in and approached him. He folded his arms across his chest and drew in a long breath. "We have a situation here. In all likelihood, a couple of men are dead in the icefall. There are several severely injured, and no one knows where the Germans are yet."

"I know it's bad," Blake offered.

"The next twenty-four hours are crucial. The injured will be brought down as quickly as possible. We'll triage and stabilize them. Some will, no doubt, need to be airlifted out."

"All right. What can I do?" Blake pushed himself up in the chair, rising to the occasion.

"You?" Dad grabbed a chair and sat next to Blake. "You are getting out before anything else happens. That icefall is so unpredictable, and it could happen again, at any time. Hell, I probably should have my head examined for bringing you here in the first place. I made a commitment to this season. You didn't. I need you to leave."

"But Dad, I can help," Blake interrupted, pleading. "And you're going to need help."

"No!" Dad slapped his thigh with his hand. "Noel is out right now rounding up those with medical training. Several climbers are paramedics, and there'll be plenty of help once we get the injured off the ice."

Blake's anger rose as he said louder than he should have, "So what? I'm just supposed to get a ride back on the next helicopter?"

"No, we can't spare the room. Besides, I want you gone before the guys come down from the icefall. Ang's agreed to get you off the mountain, and we've arranged to meet in Katmandu when the climb's over."

"Ang? Katmandu? That's insane!" Blake jumped up from the chair with such force that the chair careened backwards.

"Blake, I'm your father and I make the decisions around here. I'm doing what's best for you. This event changes everything. The climb will be changed forever. You've never been around death." His father got up from his chair and walked to the door. Turning he added, "I've seen it before. There's before the accident and then there's life after it. This is no place for a kid! Get packed. You have an hour. Ang will meet you at the hut."

Blake simmered with anger. He had come halfway around the globe to be with his father and at the first sign of trouble, he had to leave. *Not fair, just not fair. I could help. He thinks I'm a kid, a baby, who can't take it. He's wrong. He's so wrong.* Blake threw a pen across the room. It smacked the wall and fell to the floor. That was how he felt, as if he had been thrown and smashed into a wall.

Still seething, Blake made his way to the hut to retrieve his gear. He thought about what the next few weeks might bring. Backpacking with a Sherpa across Nepal did not appeal to him. He decided that once he got near a phone, he was going to call Mom.

She'd get him home fast. That would end the trekking and the possibility of a reunion with Dad in Katmandu. After this, he wasn't sure he ever wanted to talk to Dad again.

He fantasized that in years to come, Dad would regret sending him off like this.

Blake hoisted his pack up onto his back and realized he had left Dawa's camera in the medical hut. He considered leaving it there since it would just be excess weight in his back. *What good is an antique, non-functioning camera on a high country hike?* Then he remembered the pride that shown on Dawa's face when he had presented it to him. Sighing, Blake went back to get it.

Just outside the door, he saw Ang making his way toward him. His smile had not come back, and deep furrows cut across his forehead, making him look older. His stride under the weight of his pack differed little from his usual pace. Blake felt the weight on his own back and wondered how far they'd walk with the sun setting fast.

"You are ready?" Ang said.

"Just need one thing I left back with Dad," Blake said with exaggerated exasperation. He didn't mean to take his frustration out on Ang, and he immediately regretted the sarcastic tone he used.

Ang raised his left eyebrow and said, "Good. I will meet you at the chorten."

Standing in front of the hut, Dad scanned the campsite. Blake regretted his decision to fetch the camera. He hoped to bypass Dad and not even say good-bye. Now with Dad inconveniently positioned at the door, there would be no avoiding it. Dad's eyes rested on Blake, and Blake realized he was looking for him.

"Need that camera," Blake said as he brushed past Dad.

He dumped his backpack on the floor and unzipped it. He snatched the camera from the shelf, feeling its weight again, shook his head and threw it into the pack. The force of the throw bounced the camera out of the pack and onto the floor.

"Damn thing!" Blake said.

Dad came up behind him.

"Blake, I know you're upset. Things weren't supposed to go like this. This was supposed to be our time together to work things out. Sometimes life's not fair."

"Jeez, like I don't know that!" Blake interrupted. "Just forget about it." He placed the camera in the pack and scooped it up. He headed for the door and under his breath, he said, "Just forget I'm your son." He didn't look back. He just headed away from Dad, feeling his power in the moment.

Blake felt the force of Dad's grip as he was spun around to meet his father's intense eyes. "I don't need this right now. Grow up! There are men dead and dying out there. All I'm asking is that you go with Ang for a while. I'll meet you in Katmandu, I promise."

"Yeah, right!"

"Here, take this." Dad squeezed a wad of Nepalese rupees into Blake's fist.

Blake ripped free and stormed off. He readjusted the weight on his back and trudged to the chorten.

In silence, two small figures walked southwest. They passed one of the many garbage piles that surrounded Base Camp, stepping over frozen human excrement. Wrinkling his nose, Blake wondered how bad it would get. His father seemed to trust Ang, but then what did his father know?

After a few minutes of walking Blake paused and turned around. He could still see Base Camp, and he half expected his father to run after him to apologize. But no, that wouldn't happen. He knew Dad didn't really care. If he had, he wouldn't be sending him away. Blake kicked a rock at his feet. He reached down and grabbed a handful of stones and hurled them, one at a time, as hard as he could. He saw Ang still walking, getting farther ahead of him, and ran to catch up.

A mile or so into the forced march, the trail widened enough for Blake to walk beside Ang. He hurried to the Sherpa's side.

"Where are we going?" Blake asked.

Ang shifted the pack on his back and said matter-of-factly, "We will go to Tengboche, then we will see."

"Tengboche? What's that?"

"A monastery. We will find food and shelter there."

Blake shifted the pack higher on his back. "When are we supposed to be in Katmandu? I have to meet my father at some point."

"Katmandu—in June. First, Tengboche." Ang straightened under the weight of the pack and launched forward, quickening his pace.

Blake followed, but already his breathing was hampered. Tramping down a mountain did not help acclimatization. He drew in long, deep, icy breaths while his lungs burned and his throat itched. All the while he struggled to keep his mouth moist. Blake carried water but resisted the urge to take a drink. So far, Ang had not rested or taken a drink, and he vowed to follow his example.

Blake stepped behind Ang as they neared the edge of a rough glacier. Surefooted, Ang didn't hesitate as he maneuvered his way through the rippled ice almost instinctively. Struck by the vast size of the frozen river, Blake tried to keep pace with Ang. But as his breathing became more labored and his gasps for breath more audible, Ang slowed. In the distance, the snowy ridges of Kala Patar chiseled into the sky.

"I am sorry, Blake. We do not have to rush," Ang said.

"How far do we need to get today?" Blake asked.

"We do not want to sleep outside tonight, so we must get to Gorak Shep. Keeping a good pace, we will need two more hours."

A shiver ran through Blake as he realized that another two hours on the trail would mean they'd be trekking in darkness. Although the Himalayas were stark and forbidding some of the time, the sunshine always tempered those qualities. He didn't look forward to being out wandering alone at night. But then, he wouldn't be alone. Ang was there, and after all Ang was an expert. Then he remembered that the Sherpas caught in the avalanche had also been experts. Blake pushed the thought from his mind.

Once they crossed the glacier, Ang pointed to several rocks as a place to rest. Blake appreciated the well-deserved break. By now, his throat no longer itched; it was sore. Ang served up hot tea from a Thermos, and Blake eagerly downed it, soothing his raw throat. Blake dug in his pack and produced two energy bars. Ang nodded his thanks. They sat only long enough to eat and drink. Blake understood the importance of getting back on the trail.

The terrain changed dramatically as they pushed west into the last rays of the setting sun. High peaks shaded the valley, producing bone-chilling temperatures. A morass of boulders lay in front of them, and Blake imagined giants playing marbles in spirited competitions. Forced to travel around, over, and in between the stones, Ang carefully led Blake through the rock maze. Reaching relatively flat ground, Blake sensed a change in elevation confirmed by the slightly easier time he had breathing and by the shooting pain he felt in his shins from descending. Strange shadows bounced off the huge stones as Ang forced them deeper into the altered reality of light and shadow. Blake prayed they'd be through this area before they were plunged into total darkness.

At last, Ang reached into his pack and retrieved a high-powered flashlight. He cast the beam out in front of him and moved it from side to side. Blake stayed no more than two strides behind Ang due to the scarcity of light. The boulders became harder to maneuver over, but finally Blake could see straight ahead. He sighed in relief.

Ang pointed excitedly to something in the distance. Blake squinted and could see the outline of a small building. Against a black sky, ashen smoke billowed from the chimney.

"Gorak Shep!" Ang shouted.

Chapter Nine

"How much farther?" Blake asked. In the darkness, the building had seemed close, but the blackness of the night seemed to distort everything.

"Not far now," Ang answered.

The exhaustion of the day spread over Blake as he trudged for the lodging. Each time he lifted a foot, it felt heavier. The stone hut built into the side of a hill seemed oceans away even though it was only a hundred yards distant now. Perhaps exhilarated by the sight of shelter, Ang sped up, leaving Blake several steps behind. Even as their separation grew, Blake could still see Ang carrying a lone light across the open field. Blake forced himself on.

Ang stopped and waited. Blake tried to stagger a bit faster to catch up, but then he realized that Ang was not waiting for him. Caught in the torch beam stood the largest black dog Blake had ever seen. Raised hackles ran along the rigid, taut body. The dog's lips drew back in a snarl and Blake could hear a monstrous, low growl emanate from the beast. Ang cast the beam of light to the ground. As he did so, the dog barked twice but held its ground.

Even standing slightly behind Ang, Blake felt the terror of their predicament. Safety lay beyond a dog as big as a donkey who threatened to attack with the rustle of a muscle.

In the faintest voice possible, Blake whispered, "Can we distract him?"

"Hmm," came the reply.

What does 'Hmm' mean? Are we just going to stand here then? Blake thought about the food in his pack. Maybe with food he could change the dynamics of the situation. Behind Ang and hidden from the dog, he slid his hand to the pack and eased the zipper open a crack. The dog's ears pricked up, his nose wrinkled back, and he growled menacingly as he took a step toward the noise. Blake froze. It wasn't working.

Blake felt his body gain strength as he faced this new threat. His heart raced and he fought to control his breathing. If the dog did attack, they would have to fight. But fight with what? They had walking sticks, but they were folded up in their packs. They had the packs and they could use them to defend themselves.

Ten feet, perhaps, separated them from the two-hundred-pound giant. If it charged, they would have only seconds to swing the packs off their shoulders and fight back. Stiff-legged, the dog took two steps and began to close the distance, snarling all the while. Blake saw thick globs of saliva drip from the dog's mouth. He dropped his shoulder, praying that the dog wouldn't see the movement.

Shattering the concentration of the moment came cries of "Kipa! Kipa!"

Instantaneously, the dog cocked its ears backward and then shot off into the night.

Blake shook with fear as he managed to say, "Will he come back?"

"I do not think so. Chhetan must have gotten a new dog since I was last here."

Ang and Blake resumed their trek toward the hut.

"Chhetan?" Blake asked.

"Yes, this is Chhetan's home. A dog can be good protection out here."

Arriving at the hut, Blake watched an odd interchange between Ang and the Sherpa known as Chhetan. Illuminated by a fire behind him, a tall man stood in the low doorway, waiting for them. Excitement lit his face, and he began to move his tongue in and out in a way that made Blake think he was having a fit. Blake shot a quizzical glance at Ang.

Ang broke into a big smile, "Do not worry. It is just our greeting showing there are no lies on our tongues."

Ang commenced the same tongue wagging behavior. When the men drew close, Ang threw his arms around Chhetan, and the two embraced.

Dressed in an assortment of layered clothing of every color, Blake wondered if Chhetan had on everything he owned. Ang disappeared into the massive arms of the Sherpa who pounded happily on his back while the two exchanged greetings.

Finally, Ang broke free. "This is Chhetan, a cousin of mine. Chhetan, this is Blake. I am to take him on to the city."

Chhetan brought his hands together as if in prayer and said with a very formal display, "I am pleased to know you. May the Jewel in the Lotus watch over your journey."

"Thank you," Blake replied.

Chhetan led them into a large room with a low ceiling. A crackling fire billowed thick smoke that made Blake cough. Exposed beams lined the roof, and a few pieces of rudimentary furniture were scattered about. Chhetan closed the front door as far as it would go. Cracks in the door allowed some smoke to escape, but Blake noticed there was no chimney to vent the acrid fumes.

Ang and Chhetan seated themselves near the fire. Blake took a seat farthest away from the current pulling the smoke out into the night. From his vantage point, Blake watched as the door moved slightly. A sudden bump pushed the door ajar several inches. Another hit and the door flew open, and in walked the shaggy monster they had encountered previously. Blake was about to jump to his feet and grab a nearby broom for protection when Chhetan laughed and pushed the door closed again. He didn't seem alarmed, so Blake tried not to overreact.

"Chhetan, your beast accosted us on the trail! Can it be trusted?" Ang asked.

Chhetan rubbed the dog's head and gazed into its brown eyes as he said, "You are a good guard. Sometimes too good. Yes, Kipa? You threatened my friends. Such insolence!"

Ang shook his head as he watched the man baby talk to the donkey-sized canine.

"She is a good girl, really. Protective though. Now that she knows you are my friends, she will be friendly. You will see."

The dog showed none of its previous aggression. Contentedly, it sniffed the new arrivals and then settled down by the door. Chhetan bustled about the room, preparing butter tea and soup. Ang and Blake were too tired even to carry on a conversation.

Blake rested his back against the stuccoed wall and folded his legs beneath him, glad to be rid of his pack. In the smoky room, he soon drifted off. The wafting aroma of simmering meat roused him from his slumber. A bowl had been placed in front of him.

"What's this?" Blake asked pointing to the bowl.

"Yak soup. Try it, it is good," Ang said.

Blake gulped down soup while the men talked in their Sherpa tongue. Ang seemed to enjoy catching up with his cousin, because much laughter and an occasional good-natured shove accompanied their discussion.

At one point, their talk lost its merriment. Chhetan jumped to his feet apparently re-enacting something that had happened to him. Ang watched and nodded solemnly now and then, engrossed in the tale. Chhetan frantically jabbed his hand toward the ceiling indicating something taller than himself. Then he moved around the room, upright and slightly ape-like. The phrase Blake kept picking up was 'mih teh'.

Blake leaned in toward Ang. "What's 'mih teh'?"

"Mih teh is a large creature the size of a man or a little bigger," Ang said.

Chhetan jumped in front of Blake. He tugged at the skin of his cheeks. Puzzled, Blake looked to Ang for explanation.

Ang interpreted the body language. "On his face, mih teh has red fur. Sometimes he attacks man. Chhetan came across one on the high plains last week. He says that he is lucky to have escaped with his life."

"Attacks man? Mih teh is a ...bear?" Blake asked, trying to make sense of the story.

"No! No bear. Yeti." Ang said it quietly, with almost religious awe.

"Yeti? You're telling me that Chhetan saw a yeti?"

"A kind of yeti, yes. Now Chhetan is afraid because yeti brings misfortune. Already he has lost a goat."

"Ang, I've read about yeti. No one has ever found any evidence that they exist. Sure, there are tracks, but most people think they're animal tracks that melt into strange shapes.

Even the fur and bone relics have been found to be fakes. You can't believe that Chhetan saw a yeti! He must have seen a bear."

"Blake, Sherpas know that there are three kinds of yeti. We do not need your evidence. We know our land and our history. They are here, just as you are here."

Stung by the separation between himself and Ang, Blake stared into the face of a stranger. Circumstances threw the two of them together, but they were not alike. Blake felt pity as he eyed the middle-aged man stuck in his myths. Scientific tools and technology prevailed on a climb, but off the mountain, Ang lived in darkness.

After that, each of them retreated into his own corner, no one moving far from the fire. Kipa bedded down near her master, and Blake grinned while the beast snored. Saliva hung from her mouth, blowing like a spider's web in a breeze.

During the night, Blake woke up with a sudden urge to urinate. Crossing his legs, he tried to ignore it. He didn't like the idea of having to go out into the cold, pitch black night. Rolling onto his side, he willed the call of nature away. It didn't work. Finally, he got up and pushed the heavy door open. Glancing into the darkness, he struggled to make out any landmarks that might guide him. Total cloud cover prevented him from seeing by the light of the moon or stars.

"Damn it," Blake said, as he shuffled out, blind. "Just a little light would be nice."

Ten feet. I'm going to go out ten feet and take care of business. It's not safe to go stumbling about in the dark. I could easily fall off a cliff.

At the designated point, Blake unzipped and relieved himself. As he zipped up again, he heard a snort and some pawing at the ground, off to his right. His mind immediately went to Chhetan's yeti. Alone in the darkness, somewhere in the Himalayas, Blake tried to summon the scientific argument he'd used to dismiss the yeti. Frozen to the ground, Blake had to overcome his paralysis in order to turn in the direction of the noise. Another snort and Blake faced the unknown animal. Getting his bearings, he realized that the sounds were coming from the animal shed. Chhetan must own yaks. Ang had only mentioned goats. There must be farm animals kept inside the structure off the main house. Relieved, Blake tottered back inside.

Several times that night, he sat bolt upright struggling for breath. The first time he sat up, he hit his head on some drying yak meat that hung from the low ceiling. After a few more panic attacks over his breathing, Blake eventually turned on his side and mentally told himself to calm down and take deep breaths. Confused and desperate thoughts drew him back to Base Camp.

Into The Land of Snows | 51

Had everyone been rescued, and did anyone die? How was Dad handling things? Did he regret sending Blake away?

By morning Blake had forgotten the scare he had had alone in front of the lodge. His restless night left him tired, and he wondered when he'd be fully acclimatized. After sharing a quick breakfast with Chhetan, Ang and Blake packed to leave.

Outside, Blake eased his pack into position and then glanced into the animal shed. Just as he had thought. He saw a black yak chewing her cud. She raised her head and snorted when she noticed Blake. He chuckled. *OK, you scared me last night, but you're not a yeti. Not by a long shot!*

Waiting for Ang to say good-bye to Chhetan, Blake noticed with horror that stacked in front of the lodge, about ten feet from the door, was a pile of yak hides. His cheeks burned with embarrassment when he recognized that he'd peed on them in the dark. Excitedly, Kipa ran around the pile taking in the new scent.

Chhetan and Ang finally emerged into the light of the early morning Himalayan sun.

"Kipa! Kipa!" Chhetan called the dog to his side.

After waving good-bye, Ang and Blake walked south.

"Where to?" Blake asked.

"To the village of Lobuche and then on to Duglha."

Chapter Ten

Blake walked alongside Ang that morning. "How do you think they're doing back at camp?" Blake asked.

Ang shrugged. "It is difficult to say. We are not there and, therefore, we cannot be of help. It is best not to think about it now."

Heading due south and descending with every step, the two made good time over the rocky terrain. The morning sun warmed them from the left. Blake's muscles ached, but somehow it felt good to be moving. His breathing became rhythmic as his body responded to the new day of trekking.

At the first rest stop, Blake pulled on his headset while Ang swigged water. The scenery of the Himalayas would be improved by the beat of some good music. Ang wasn't much of a talker, anyway.

By the time the village of Lobuche came into sight, the heel on Blake's right foot hurt. He chastised himself silently for not putting on two pairs of socks. He found that if he slowed down and took smaller steps he didn't need to raise his boot so high. That in turn saved his heel from rubbing against the back of the boot. Deliberately, he breathed harder so Ang would slow down.

"Foot hurt?" Ang asked.

"Nah, I'm okay." *How does he know about my foot? I haven't been limping.* A few steps in front of Ang, Blake forced himself to move faster, but then winced at the pain. Luckily, Ang couldn't see his facial expression.

Three clustered lodges sat huddled together in front of them, just off the trail. Tied near the door of the trading post stood a yak-like creature.

"I thought yaks were bigger than that. Is that a baby?" Blake asked whisking off his earphones.

"No yak, no baby. That is a dzo. Mother cow and father yak."

The beast eyed them casually as they went into the store. Blake bent at the waist to avoid hitting his head on the low doorway, but Ang passed through without difficulty.

A small Sherpa woman swung a prayer wheel and chanted behind a counter. Dressed in the traditional chuba robe, with her eyes closed, she had not noticed when Blake and Ang entered. Blake thought it peculiar that someone would be praying at work. Respectfully, Ang approached her but did not interrupt.

Blake's eyes adjusted within moments to the darkness of the shop. In a corner, a dung fire burned, filling the room with heavy smoke. Shelves, from the floor to the ceiling, displayed gear for trekkers. Food items lined the walls behind the woman.

Animated laughter erupted behind a drawn curtain. Ang swooshed the drape to the side, revealing a man bouncing a baby on his lap. Startled, the man drew the baby to his chest, but quickly relaxed seeing Ang.

"Ang Thondup! How good to see you," the man said, rising to his feet.

"And you. This is the new little one?"

"Ah, yes. My greatest joy." The man turned the baby around for Ang's inspection.

Ang took the baby's hand and the little one wrapped its tiny fingers around his index finger.

"I thought you would be carrying this time of year, not babysitting," Ang joked.

"I go out next week with American trekkers. And I will miss her," the man answered, sliding the baby to his hip.

Surprised to see such a tender exchange between dedicated outdoorsmen, Blake turned back to see the woman at the counter put down her prayer wheel and approach them. Greetings were exchanged, and the woman reached for the child. Embraced by her mother's arms, the baby grabbed the simple beaded necklace that hung on the woman's chest.

The men, including Blake, retreated behind the curtain where Ang's friend offered them homemade beer. Blake accepted a mug of warm chang and Ang didn't even raise an eyebrow.

Soon the men began to talk in Sherpa, which left Blake wondering what was being said. As he sipped his warm, pungent beer, a feeling of comfortable euphoria swept over him. Several cues in the dialogue made him believe the two were recounting tales of their past, and there were a few times when the conversation grew quiet and then erupted in laughter. Certain he was missing some racy conversation, Blake wished he knew Sherpa. Offered a second mug of beer, he didn't refuse.

When Ang's friend tried to fill Blake's mug for the third time, Ang cupped a hand down on the mug and shook his head. Blake wasn't angry, and maybe he felt slightly relieved. Shuffling his feet, he remembered that his heel needed attention. It would be best to see to that without an audience.

"Thanks," Blake said, shaking the mug as he got up.

A little unsteady on his feet, he stumbled through the curtain heading for the door. He couldn't remember the last time he felt this happy. The Dzo snorted, and Blake thought he saw the animal raise a disapproving eyebrow. *Was that possible?*

He sat on a rock safely out of range of the Dzo. The midday sun blasted its rays down on Blake's back. He unlaced his boot and eased it carefully off. Bright red blood soaked his sock at the heel. Wincing, he gingerly removed it. The heel stung in the crisp air, having been rubbed raw. Blake turned out the contents of his pack to find the few medical supplies he carried. The old camera Dawa had given him tumbled to the ground. Picking it up, Blake noticed that some letters were scratched along the side. He'd never seen it before, but as he ran his finger along the side he saw that it said 'H. SOMERVELL.' Apparently, H. Somervell had lost the camera on Everest a long time ago.

Casting the camera aside, Blake placed a large band-aid over his wound and wrapped gauze around it for extra protection. Two pairs of heavy socks finished off the job. He stood up, moved his injured foot in the boot, and found he would be able to walk without pain. Ang came up behind him and handed him a wad of desiccated meat.

"Jerky. It is a good, fast meal," Ang stated.

"Doesn't look too good." Blake turned the dry, brown matter over in his hand.

"That is illusion." Ang bit off a chunk and made exaggerated sounds of contentment.

As the two trekked away from the lodge, Blake forced himself to try the jerky. His teeth had a thorough workout as the spicy, smoky flavors permeated his taste buds.

Blake swallowed the masticated bit of jerky. "You're right, Ang. It's pretty good. Is it beef?"

"No. No beef up here. It is yak," Ang said.

"I guess that makes sense. What did you mean when you said 'That is illusion'?"

"We shall have to have a very long talk about that. It makes me recall my time at the monastery."

Blake pushed a partially chewed hunk of jerky into his cheek. "You were a monk?" he asked incredulously.

"From the age of seven to fifteen, I lived at monastery. My father carried for high altitude then and we had money. I left to help my mother and sisters after he died."

Stunned, Blake became silent. He concentrated on eating the rest of the meat as he wrestled with the apparent contradiction. The man he had just drunk beer with and heard tell dirty jokes didn't seem like a monk. Still, spending eight years in a monastery must have had some effect.

The wind picked up and gray clouds moved in from the east. The afternoon took on a somber tone, and Blake shivered in the breeze as they trudged on. Determined to find out more from Ang, he started the conversation. "We have lots of time, so tell me about illusion."

"Illusion?" Ang said and paused. "Illusion encompasses all our ordinary perceptions that are deformed by our ignorance," he answered as if reciting a poem he had memorized.

Blake felt a strange sense of familiarity in the way the talk began. At home, he and Slade often debated different topics. Slade always started with a firm statement about something, and then they would explore the topic for hours. Sometimes the initial statement would be rejected, and sometimes it was accepted. Often Blake and Slade would accept the statement with many clarifications.

"Okay, perceptions are based on knowledge we get through our senses. What we see, hear, taste, smell, and touch. Right?" Blake said.

"Yes, but it also may involve past experience or other insight."

Blake nodded. "Now, what about ignorance? How are we ignorant?"

"By this, we mean an erroneous way of thinking that advances the idea that beings and things are real, independent, solid, and intrinsic."

"So people and stuff, or matter...isn't real?"

Ang paused again. "Things exist or are real, but not in the ways we usually think. Appearances are illusionary. We must look beyond them."

Blake nodded and tried to make sense of it all.

"All right, so like this glove," Blake said, holding up his covered hand. "I can see this glove. I can feel this glove. The glove is real, but...?"

Ang stopped and, with great patience, cupped his hand around the glove. "This glove is a phenomenon. It appears in your mind through your perceptions of seeing and feeling. What you know to be this glove are its appearances. Its true nature is emptiness."

"How can it be empty? I can feel it."

Ang smirked. "Yes, I know. It is often hard to understand new ways of seeing things."

Three stone huts came into view in a valley just ahead of them. On the hills beyond, Blake could see several yaks grazing on sparse blue-gray vegetation. He wondered how such large creatures could survive on the limited vegetation of the area.

"Is that Duglha?" Blake asked.

"Yes. We will stay here tonight. Tomorrow, we will travel on to the monastery."

As Blake and Ang walked into town, they saw villagers busy with their daily chores. Children dashed about playing tag games. A man tending goats came forward to welcome them and ushered them into his home. Ang knew the family and soon they were seated before a smoky fire, sharing tea. From a television program about Tibet he had seen, Blake recognized the drink to be butter tea. Politely, he tasted the salty, fatty mixture and winced as the hot liquid flowed down his throat. Butter tea was definitely an acquired taste.

Blake listened to the conversation, conducted totally in the Sherpa language, as if it were a song. He enjoyed the strangeness of the sounds as they rolled over the family's tongues. Ang would translate a phrase or sentence here or there so Blake could keep up with what was being said.

After tea, Ang motioned Blake toward the door.

They stepped out into the late afternoon sun, and Ang pointed to a ridgeline a short walk from the village. "I want to show you something."

The two climbed a rocky, snow-covered incline as they made their way out of the village. Almost at the top, Blake saw a ridge, lined with rough, stone chortens.

"Is this an ancient site, Ang?"

"No." Ang shook his head. "It is a modern site. These monuments were built for Sherpas who died on Everest. In the next few weeks, villagers will add more for those lost in the latest avalanche."

Within seconds, a cloud from the neighboring valley floated in and settled over them. The monuments to the dead, lost in the fog, were the same as the men, lost to their families. Ang closed his eyes, chanting a prayer. Blake turned away, feeling empty.

Chapter Eleven

Stiff from lying on the floor all night, Blake stretched and got up. Ang, sitting near the fire, smiled and nodded as he sipped from a clay cup. The sound of heavy hoof beats and clanging bells drew Blake to the hut's door. Edging it open, he peered into the early morning light. A line of yaks, loaded down with supplies, plodded its way through the village. Ten or so Sherpas and Western trekkers accompanied the yaks.

Ang joined Blake at the door. "We should leave soon. It is a long walk to Tengboche. Come eat something."

Ang spooned a gray gruel into a small bowl and Blake ate the tasteless cereal. A hot cup of tea warmed him and soothed away some of his aches. After the quick breakfast, Blake stowed his gear and they prepared to leave.

"Aren't we going to say good-bye to the family?" Blake asked.

"No. They have left for the high meadows to feed the livestock. I have already expressed our appreciation for their hospitality."

Dawn in the valley did not bring the intense sun Blake had grown used to. His sunglasses stayed tucked in his pocket, and he wondered if the low haze would ever burn off. Heavy with moisture, the air felt strange on his skin.

They made their way down a sloping hillside where the trail cut next to a deep river. The deafening roar of the current prevented them from talking, but the well-kept trail allowed them to descend rapidly. Gradually, the path left the riverside and crossed over into another valley.

Clapping a hand on Blake's shoulder and pointing, Ang said, "There. That is Pheriche."

Another small settlement lay ahead of them. Blake realized it was a landmark to Ang, even though it was no more impressive than the other settlements. As they neared the village, he saw commercial establishments where signs in several languages hawked goods for sale.

Ang showed no hesitation as he ducked into a tea shop. Blake plopped down on a stone bench and reached for his water bottle. As his stomach grumbled, he glanced at his watch. It was nearly noon. No wonder he was hungry.

Ang emerged from the shop and handed Blake a square of milky, white cheese. "Churpi, yak cheese," he said.

Blake lifted the cheese to his nose and inhaled. It had a mild, flavorful scent. He took a bite and found it to be quite delicious. In the few moments they stood outside eating, the wind picked up. Droplets of water crystallized and stung Blake's cheeks. The day grew darker as a storm brewed.

"We must go down to get out of the weather," Ang said, pointing south.

Blake swallowed the last morsel of cheese and tightened his hood around his face. Heads down, they moved away from the storm. Descending several hundred feet removed them from the ferocity of the swirling ice and snow. The wind died and blue skies stretched before them. Soon the canyon widened, revealing Alpine meadows.

The valley that stretched before them was almost indescribably beautiful. They strolled through the green countryside until they reached the other side. Happy to take a break, Blake dug in his backpack to retrieve his camera. He lifted Dawa's camera out of the pack so he could rummage for his own camera more efficiently.

Ang squatted and picked up the ancient camera. "What is this?"

"It's just something Dawa gave me. I gave him a book and he gave me that."

Blake grasped his digital camera and stood to take several shots. The storm still raged to the north, and he snapped that. Slowly, he faced each of the cardinal directions and clicked photos. He finished and was surprised to see Ang still holding the old camera, carefully turning it over again and again. The respect Ang showed Dawa's gift seemed immense. It was, after all, just an old camera.

"Do you like old cameras?" Blake asked.

"It is a very old camera. Do you know the name 'H. Somervell'?"

"No. He must have lost that a long time ago, though."

With reverence, Ang traced his finger over the rough letters. A moment or two passed before he looked up and resumed the conversation. "H. Somervell may have been Howard Somervell, surgeon and member of the 1924 British expedition to Everest."

"The one with Mallory?" Blake asked, dropping to his knees, suddenly interested in the black box.

"Yes. It is the most famous mystery in all mountaineering. George Mallory and Andrew Irvine were last seen heading to the summit. When they failed to return to camp, they vanished into legend. No one knows what happened to them and there is still speculation that they may have summited Everest decades before Hillary and Norgay."

"But wasn't Mallory's body found recently?" *I read that in one my travel books.*

"Correct. In 1999, a research team did find and identify Mallory's body. Everyone hoped that a camera he carried would be recovered, but it was not with the body. Even now, there are international teams looking for the camera in the hope of settling for all time the question of who first climbed to the top of the world."

Blake shook with excitement. "Are you saying *this* is that camera?"

"Perhaps it is so." Ang gently placed the camera into Blake's outstretched hands.

Flabbergasted, Blake held the camera with a new sense of respect.

"So there might be film still in it? Film that could be developed, even after all these years?" Blake asked. He cradled the camera against his chest.

Ang nodded. "So it has been thought. When we reach the monastery, I will introduce you to a man who knows much about cameras. Until then, carry it carefully."

Blake nodded, and with unsteady hands, he wrapped Dawa's gift in a soft, white T-shirt and packed it gently into his backpack. To think he might be carrying the answer to a mystery that had held the world captive for over eighty years was a heady experience.

Of course, it might not be the right camera and even if it is, the film may be ruined. It might be worthless, just a relic of an expedition gone wrong. But if it was with Mallory and Irvine on the climb, then it still would have historical importance. *What if it shows Mallory standing on the summit of Everest? Now that would be awesome! What would Dad think if I solve the mystery once and for all?*

With each new insight, Blake's sense of excitement rose. He didn't even notice the progress he and Ang were making along the trail. The path clung tightly to the river Imja Khola. This time the water's noise only heightened Blake's exuberant mood. A few hours later, they approached an old and weathered monastery. Large, carved stones greeted them just outside the settlement.

"Ang, what are these?" Blake asked as he ran his hand over a moss-covered stone.

"Those we call mani stones. Each contains a prayer."

Blake took a step back to see the entire stone all at once. The strange symbols painstakingly carved into the hard rock represented a huge investment of time and energy, and the sheer quantity of stones made them an impressive sight. How long did it take to do this, Blake wondered.

Just ahead, the scattered buildings of the monastery sat midway up the valley.

"We will not be able to stay here if we are to make Tengboche by nightfall," Ang explained. "However, I thought you might like to know about the relics."

"What relics?"

"The monks of Pangboche Monastery are custodians of yeti relics. There is a scalp and a skeletal hand," Ang said, appearing confident that this would impress his skeptical friend.

"Oh, yeah? And you've seen them?"

"Yes, on several occasions, I have had the good fortune to see them."

"I read about the scalp. Some European scientist found it to be a fake. And the hand probably is too. Interesting to know that they're both here, though," Blake said.

Ang shook his head. They pushed on, skirting the terraced village of Pangboche just below the monastery. The rough hillsides were covered in coarse vegetation that reminded Blake of the American southwest. The trail cut west and crossed the Imja Khola. Ahead lay a plank bridge swaying in the afternoon breeze.

Blake hesitated. "We have to cross that?"

"Yes. It is quite safe. I have crossed many times."

Blake didn't gain confidence from Ang's words. As they drew closer, he could see that there were gaps in the planks of the bridge's flooring. A deep river current ran only feet from the bottom of the bridge. The river's spray misted the planks, making them shiny.

In the lead, Ang reached the entrance to the bridge and called back, "I will go first. When I am in the middle, I will signal you to come. You come slow. Yes?"

Blake's stomach did a flip-flop, but he nodded anyway, trying to look tough.

Ang put his hands on the guide ropes and hopped up onto the bridge, showing no fear. Hand, foot, hand, foot, he made his way across it. The bridge swayed violently, seeming to revolt against anyone crossing. Ang looked like a spider ambling across a web.

At the halfway mark, the bridge strained and dipped low, supporting Ang's weight. Ang turned and signaled. Blake felt his heart beat in his chest. *If he can do it, so can I. Get a grip!*

Blake forced his hands to the ropes. He pulled himself up and looked down. The river raced with more intensity than he had imagined. If he fell, he would certainly be swept away to his death. *Don't look down. Hand, foot, Hand, foot!*

He wanted to focus on Ang, but he had to watch his footing. There were places in the bridge where he had to take an extra-large step to get over a hole. He found that moving hand and foot was not the most difficult aspect. The hard part was dealing with the sway of the bridge every time he advanced. If only the bridge had been secured with one girder sunk deep into the river's floor, the task would have been a cakewalk. He imagined exactly where he would have placed this support.

Momentarily distracted, looking beyond his feet, he misjudged the distance over one of the gaps in the flooring. His right foot barely made contact with the next plank. He felt his foot slip backward off the slick bridge and plunge downward. Blake screamed. The force of the misstep dislodged his right hand from its grip. He fell.

Chapter Twelve

"Do not panic!" Ang shouted.

With the roar of the water, Blake heard nothing distinguishable.

Ang released his grip on the guide ropes, and the extra slack allowed Blake to hold on with his left hand. Down on his left knee, Blake's whole right side swung free beneath the bridge. Spray from the river licked at his face. He grunted and threw his right hand toward the guide rope. Catching it, he gritted his teeth and pulled himself up. His right foot made contact near the left. Huffing and puffing, he glanced toward Ang. Ang resumed his hold on the ropes and nodded. Slowly, Ang moved across the bridge, and Blake followed.

Several hours later, the pair walked through the forest surrounding Tengboche. Blake pointed to a clearing where young fanged musk deer frolicked. He stopped to hear the muffled calls of a bird he didn't recognize.

"Danphe," Ang said, pointing.

Blake saw a beautiful pheasant with sparkling, iridescent plumage under an evergreen tree. The sight of the exotic creatures and the change in landscape comforted Blake as they made their way to the monastery complex.

Ang didn't hesitate at a fork in the trail. He cut right.

"Why are we going around? Can't we follow this trail?" Blake asked.

"This is your first time to Tengboche, the most beautiful place in the world. You must see it as it was meant to be seen. The mountains frame the monastery. Have patience."

Blake shook his head and rolled his eyes, all behind Ang's back. *What difference can it possibly make? Jeez, if we cut through the back, I'll still be able to see the mountains behind the monastery. It's not like either one is going to move.*

The pack on Blake's back felt heavier than it had when they set out. He trudged along, hoping that by conceding to Ang's desire to take the long way around this time, he might have some leverage in influencing other decisions along the way. So far, Ang had called all the shots. *Maybe he will ask me what I want to do once in a while and I can voice my opinions. That might be hard though, since Ang's so used to being in charge. He thinks I'm a kid he's babysitting.*

As they circled the settlement, Blake noticed a large building in the center, surrounded by many smaller structures. The front of the monastery came into view. Sitting atop a hill, the three-story, massive stone building could be reached by a carefully constructed stairway. It was far more impressive than any other building Blake had seen so far.

Painted red, the wooden windows and doors reminded him that Buddhists were not afraid of color.

Blake had his first view of Tengboche, the way Ang intended him to see it. He walked to the foot of the staircase and found the view breathtaking. Ang pointed to the peaks and named each one. The monastery sat on a promontory surrounded by the high peaks of Everest, Nuptse, Lhotse, and Ama Dablam. The white structure was embraced by the snow-covered mountains with their crisp ridges cutting into a cloudless, blue sky.

"You were right. It was worth the extra walk," Blake said softly.

Ang nodded as they stood together and took in the sight. A moment passed, and Ang said, "First, I must find a place for us to stay and get some food. Then, I will take you to the photographer. You look tired. Perhaps you could rest here while I make these arrangements."

"Okay, sure," Blake answered.

Ang set off, and Blake seated himself on the stairs of the monastery, reveling in the warmth of the sun's rays. Tired and hungry, he dug through his pack and found some hard candy, which soon sated his growling stomach. Off came his boots to check on the wound on his foot. The bandage remained intact, and no new blood had seeped through.

His mind drifted back to the camera, and he wondered if it could really solve the long-time mystery of Everest. Who really got to the top of the world first? Thinking of Everest reminded him of Base Camp and Dad. What if he had been able to stay? One thing was for certain, he wouldn't have been able to develop the film right away, and that meant that the mystery would remain unsolved while at camp. And if Dad had found out in all likelihood, he would have confiscated the camera, even if it had been a gift from Dawa. Blake smiled. For the first time, he felt happy to be off the mountain.

He checked his other foot and suddenly found himself in a shadow. Cast by a monk in a burgundy robe, the darkness lasted only an instant as the man hurried up the stairs.

Blake snapped a few photos of the monastery and rested comfortably until Ang returned.

"Come," Ang said. "I have found a place for us."

Ang led him to a small stone building with a flat roof. Inside, a low table was set with a simple meal of roasted yak meat that teased Blake's stomach. Flat bread and cheese lay stacked next to a pot of tsampa. They sat on the floor and dug into the meal.

"This photographer guy, is he a monk?" Blake asked.

"No. Mr. Rodney Taylor arrived here in '54 just after the British succeeded in climbing to the top of Chomolungma. He worked for a magazine then, taking photographs. Now he works on treks, guiding and helping foreigners take excellent photos of the mountains."

"Can he be trusted?"

"I believe so. He has lived here with the permission of the monastery's highest lama for nearly fifty years."

After eating, Ang took Blake to meet Mr. Rodney Taylor.

"Would you blokes like to come in?" Taylor said, with a slight British accent.

He was a tall, gray-haired man with a deeply lined face. His blue eyes lit up at the prospect of company. As he moved aside to allow them to enter, Blake caught a whiff of beer on his breath.

"Please sit," Taylor said as he gestured to an old couch near a fire. Although the room was filled with an assortment of both English and Nepalese furniture, Blake focused on the framed photos that lined the walls. Some were black and white, but most were in color and all of them were mountain landscapes.

Slowly, Blake moved to the couch and sat. Taylor rifled through some cabinets and emerged with a box. He offered them Scottish shortbread from the package. Blake grabbed one and eagerly bit into it.

Ang accepted a cookie but just held it as he said, "Mr. Taylor, Blake would like to ask your permission—"

"Now Ang, I've asked you before to call me Roddy! I'm sure you don't want me to have to resort to calling you Mr. Thundup," Taylor said as he reached for a bottle of beer.

"Yes, Roddy. I will try to remember."

"Good, good. Now what's the boy want?"

Blake spoke up. "Mr. Taylor, I'd like to borrow your darkroom. I took some pictures at Base Camp and I'd really like to get them developed. I'd like to send some back to my grandfather." *Okay, it's a lie, but just a little one. This guy doesn't care what I develop anyway. Throwing in that stuff about my grandfather might make him more likely to help me.*

Ang lowered his eyebrows and shot a look at Blake.

Hesitating, Taylor asked, "Have you worked in a darkroom before? I leave on a trek tomorrow, and I won't be here to help."

"Oh, sure. I took black-and-white photography at the community center back home."

"And there is the matter of materials. If I let everyone use my supplies, I won't have a livelihood."

Blake jumped up and pulled out the money Dad had given him. "Here, take what's fair."

Taylor removed a few bills. "Right, the darkroom is just behind that curtain. There's a key to the place just under the mat outside."

That night, Ang loaded the fire well for the long evening. All night, the flames flickered, fueling Blake's imagination. *What if there are pictures on the roll? What if Mallory and Irvine did reach the summit? Tomorrow, I might hold the answer to the mystery in my hands. But then, the camera, if it is Mallory's, has been outside exposed to some of the most severe weather on earth. How likely is it that the film will be in good condition? Even if it can be developed, there might not even be any pictures on the roll. Maybe Mallory died before the summit, in which case no pictures would have been taken. But there's always the chance something will be recoverable. What should I do if I get pictures?*

Chapter Thirteen

The next day, Blake stood in Taylor's darkroom. A battery-powered lantern provided enough light for him to memorize the positions of his tools. Before him on the rough bench lay a film cassette, can opener, film reel, tank and tank cover. His hands shook as he ran his fingers over the items. He closed his eyes and withdrew his hands. In his mind, he ran through the actions he would need to perform in total darkness. His fingers touched each item in succession.

Before he would trust himself with the 127 film from the vest pocket camera that Dawa had given him, he would practice on a roll of 35mm. That morning he and Ang met some Swedish tourists who were willing to allow Blake to develop a roll they had shot the previous day in the mountains around the monastery. It was valuable to the tourists, but it had no worldwide significance. If he ruined it, he would have to make an uncomfortable apology, but that would be the end of it. *If I can't do the 35mm roll correctly, I won't even attempt the other. I'll wait for Mr. Taylor to return.*

When he finally felt comfortable with his surroundings, he closed the darkroom door and turned off the lantern. In the blackness, Blake drew in a deep breath through his nose and held it. He let the air out slowly. *This is just like at the community center. Everything is here and I've done this lots of times.*

Carefully, he removed the film from the cassette using the can opener and loaded the film onto a plastic film reel. He then placed the reel into the film tank and covered it.

"Easy!" Blake exclaimed, snapping the lantern back on.

He skimmed through the directions on the chemical packages to refresh his memory of what to do next. Just like back home, he followed all the steps. Finally, he pulled the film from the tank and hung it to dry. The negatives showed various mountain scenes and, in a few, people were posed in typical tourist fashion.

Exhilarated by his success with the 35mm film, Blake felt confident when he reached for the vest pocket camera. He removed the film and was surprised by the narrow, long roll he found. Opening this odd-sized cassette in the dark might be tough, especially since he didn't have one to practice on. *I'll have to go slowly and be careful.*

Once again, Blake laid the materials out on the bench. He closed his eyes and felt the implements, ensuring that everything was exactly where he needed it. He clicked off the lantern. In total darkness, he picked up the cassette and reached for the opener. Sweaty hands fumbled with the tool, and it fell to the floor. Down on hands and knees, Blake searched and found the opener under the bench. He stood up and forced himself to act slowly and precisely. He wiped his hands, one at a time, on his pants and started over.

Cautiously, he opened the cassette and unwound the film. He transferred it to a film reel with great dexterity and placed it into the film tank, covering it. He sighed with relief as he turned the lantern back on.

"Okay, so far, so good."

Ready to start processing, Blake gathered the film developer, a stop bath, a fixer with hardener, and a hypo eliminator bath.

He poured the developer through the pour spout and closed it without ever opening the tank. Checking his watch, he agitated the tank, turning it upside down once every minute. He tapped the tank to remove any air bubbles that might form. Blake followed the package instructions precisely for timing the developer and then dumped the solution into an old tin.

Next, he used a specially prepared stop bath mixture to wash off the developer. The film was then treated with a fixer containing a hardener, which Blake knew would prevent the negatives from being scratched.

He moved to the dry sink, removed the tank cover, and proceeded to pour pitchers of cold water over the film. Hypo eliminator removed the fixer, and a final wash ended the process.

Holding his breath, Blake pulled the film out for his first look at the negatives. The small roll produced only eight exposures. He faced the lantern to view the images as he unrolled the coil of celluloid.

The first shadowy image showed two figures in front of a tent. No other details were discernable. He would have to print the negatives to see if the photos showed Mallory and Irvine. That would be easy enough, and the negatives seemed to be of high quality, so in all probability they would produce quality photos. With good photos, he'd be able to compare them to pictures of Mallory and Irvine in any of hundreds of climbing books. Of course, it still might not be Mallory and Irvine. It could be Somervell or even someone else.

His fingers moved to the second image. A man appeared to be climbing a wall. Taken up close with nothing in the background to serve as a landmark, the location of the photo would be hard to identify. It could be anywhere in the Himalayas, and the man was most likely not looking at the camera since he was engaged in climbing. So, in all probability, the man couldn't be identified either.

The celluloid curled into a roll as his hands moved to the third negative. *What? What's this?* Blake squinted and drew the film closer to the lantern. He moved in tighter to view the image of someone running down a hillside. *Why would a climber run down Everest? Is this Everest? Maybe. Oh, no it's not someone.... Could it be?*

As the horror seized him, he forced himself to move on to the next scene, hoping it wasn't true. His jaw dropped. The next image confirmed his thoughts. The creature. The creature had stopped, facing the camera. Holy crap, these are images of a yeti! A yeti on Everest in 1924. Un-doctored, untouched, and unreal.

Blake frantically viewed the next image, swept up in the discovery. Someone, human this time, bent over pointing to the ground. *What's he pointing to? I'll have to print it to find out. Doesn't look like much.*

Moving on Blake checked the final three negatives. All showed different views of the same mountainside. Those would also need to be printed to see if any other significant details could be seen.

It took Blake some time to find all the supplies he needed to prepare the prints properly. Mr. Taylor had some of the oldest equipment, but at least he did have some of the best papers. Several hours of hard work and rework rewarded Blake with eight 8x10 photos. More could be done with tonal control, but overall he was pleased with the black and whites and very anxious to show them to Ang.

I'll need to be careful. I can't tell just anyone. Ang can be trusted, I think. I mean eight years in a monastery—that must mean something. I won't be able to share these with anyone else. They've got to be valuable, and someone might try to steal them. I need to keep this between me and Ang until I see Dad again in Katmandu.

At midday, Tengboche Monastery bustled with activity. Blake left Mr. Taylor's house and headed out to find Ang. Various trekkers had pitched tents in the shadows of the monastery's main building, and many of them were out and about. He passed a group of men speaking French and saw some young monks replacing prayer flags. The sun rose higher and shone intensely on his back. He readjusted the folder he carried, making sure that none of the photos had slipped.

Blake entered the house Ang had rented and found him on the floor amid a pile of trekking brochures and maps. His entrance caused the maps to ripple, and Ang looked up.

"The photographs?" Ang inquired.

Blake slammed the door to ensure their privacy, and half a dozen hiking guides flew up in the breeze and slapped the wall. Ang rose and approached Blake.

"You're not going to believe this!" Blake said.

"Perhaps not. Please tell me anyway."

Blake plopped down at the low table and removed the first photo from the folder.

"Mallory and Irvine! I'm pretty sure, anyway. I'll need to check a couple of books, but it looks like them to me."

Ang sank to his knees and picked up the photo. He nodded. "I agree. I have seen many photos of the legendary climber George Mallory. I believe that is him."

"This is where it gets interesting." Blake paused for effect. His fingers danced over the edge of the folder.

"You have a photo of them on the top of Chomolungma?"

"No. I can't tell if they ever made it to the top. Maybe they did. Maybe they didn't. That mystery won't be solved by these. No, I told you that you wouldn't guess. But try. It's something else. Something just as mysterious, though. Guess!"

"I am not skilled at guessing games. Perhaps you could just show me the photos."

Blake nodded in disappointment and removed all the photos from the folder. Slowly, he laid the images, one by one, across the table so Ang could view them in their entirety.

Blake watched as Ang's eyes moved over the image of the climber at the wall and settled on the first photo of the yeti running. Ang lifted the photo to get a better look.

"Mih teh."

Blake pounded a fist on the table. "Right! Mih teh, yeti. These are the first photos of the real thing! No way did Mallory and Irvine bother with a hoax. Nothing would have been more important than going for the summit."

"Yes. They were driven men looking for their place in history." Ang scanned the photo array and then focused on the close up shot of the yeti. "He resembles the images on the tapestries and monastery walls. Mih teh is the size of a man, covered with red fur except for the face. We cannot know what color this creature is from the black-and white-photo, but its structure tells me it is not a bear. It is not dzu teh, the bear-like yeti."

"What are the three yeti creatures Sherpa believe in?" Blake asked.

Mih teh, dzo teh, and Thelma. I do not think it is Thelma because its arms do not hang down low. This is mih teh, human looking with much hair," Ang said with certainty.

"Yeti!" Blake shouted.

"Yeti." Ang answered as he reviewed the final three photos where the dark figure could be seen moving farther and farther down the mountain.

Throughout the entire exchange Ang had been interested in Blake's photos, but not excited. With Ang's confirmation that he actually had good photos of a yeti, Blake had trouble containing himself and focusing on what to do next.

Calmly, Ang gathered the photos into a pile. "What will you do with them?"

"Good question. These are valuable, really valuable." Blake stood up and began to pace about the room. "I can't do anything with them here, that's for sure. Once I get to Katmandu I can go to the press. There's got to be a way to contact the Associated Press or something. Maybe get on the internet. Dad will have some ideas."

"So you want to show the world?"

"Yeah, of course! This is big. The most famous mountain climber of all time loses a camera and dies on Everest trying to reach the top. Eighty years later the camera is found, and the recovered film shows the world its first REAL pictures of a yeti."

"Is proving to the world the existence of yeti important?" Ang asked quietly.

"Hell yes!" Blake said. "Everyone will want to know about this."

"Perhaps," Ang said. He rose and left Blake alone clutching the photos.

A minute or two passed as Blake pondered Ang's strange behavior. He had agreed with Blake that the photos showed Mallory and a yeti. Yet he showed no excitement or enthusiasm for this discovery. *Is he jealous that he doesn't have the pictures? Maybe he resents my having them.*

Blake carefully placed the photos back into the folder and slid the packet into his backpack. He left the hut, intent on finding Ang.

Chapter Fourteen

"Why are we here?" Blake whispered to Ang. In the darkened room, several butter lamps burned. The smell of incense made the room feel heavy, and Blake heard low chanting.

Ang answered in a quiet voice. "It is customary to visit the lama or Rinpoche when one arrives at the monastery."

Blake's eyes became accustomed to the light, and he noticed two monks dressed in burgundy flanking the Rinpoche. Behind an ornately painted table, the lama sat on a tall bench. In one hand he held a bell and in the other a silver-colored, dumbbell-like object. He swayed side to side, his eyes closed as he chanted and manipulated the objects. Blake scanned the room and found all the surfaces decorated. The walls were covered in elaborate paintings depicting gods and demons. The artwork was brightly colored, but the dim light kept it from being overwhelming. He dug his bare feet into a thick carpet with a geometric pattern.

As they waited, Blake reviewed the odd afternoon he had experienced. He circled the monastery grounds for over an hour without finding Ang. He had no idea where his friend had gone, and it was difficult to ask anyone for information. Many of the teams of climbers were internationals speaking a wide range of languages, but not necessarily English. Just that afternoon he had heard French, German, and Italian, and of course Sherpa and Tibetan. Finally, he sat down near the front of the monastery hoping that Ang would find him. And not long after,

Ang approached and insisted on taking him inside the main monastery building. No real explanation had been offered as to why this was important now.

The chanting ceased and the Rinpoche opened his eyes as he laid the objects on the table before him. One of the monks motioned Ang and Blake forward. Ang brought his hands together in a praying position and bowed slightly as he approached the Rinpoche. Blake, unaware of the appropriate customs to follow when meeting a lama, deferred to Ang's judgment. He bowed and tented his hands.

As they drew closer, Blake lifted his gaze from the floor to get a better look at the man seated on the altar. The lama's smile greeted Blake. He had a wrinkled face and kind brown eyes. On his head he wore a red hat shaped like a single flower petal, and a simple yellow robe flowed from his shoulders.

"Welcome to Tengboche, Blake. I am the Rinpoche."

"Thank you." Blake straightened.

"I have known your friend Ang Thondup for many years. I am happy you are in his care."

"Yes, I'm happy too."

Well, the conversation's not great, but it's kind of cool to meet the most important person around here. It's a little like meeting a mayor or something, back home. I'll bet this guy meets everyone who passes through.

"Ang has come to me on a matter of extreme importance. I have thought a great deal on this matter," the Rinpoche said as he raised his hand.

From a shelf behind the lama, one of the monks brought forth a tray. On the tray lay the 1924 Kodak and a familiar folder. This he set before the Rinpoche.

Blake glanced over at Ang, whose gaze rested on the rug.

"That's my camera!" Blake shouted. Ang cringed.

"Perhaps. The camera is not of concern to me. Take it," the lama answered.

In a defensive tone, Blake said, "And I want the photos too. It's all my stuff!"

"Ang has told me of your intentions regarding the photographs. I do not agree that releasing these will be for the benefit of all."

"Well, maybe not—but it's not your decision to make. The camera was given to me by a friend, and therefore the photos are mine to do with what I please!"

Not intimidated by Blake's combative verbalizations, the Rinpoche continued, "I agree in theory that the articles are yours. I can put forward no defensible argument to dispute this. I, however, do not agree that you are in a sufficient state of mind to make the wisest decision regarding this property."

Blake's jaw jutted forward and the words came fast. "So you agree it's my stuff, but you're going to keep it anyway? You are the highest religious person here and you're going to steal my stuff? What, because you can?"

"No. I will steal nothing. I will, instead, provide you with an opportunity. An opportunity of mind. A wager, if you like. I know you play checkers. I will hold these possessions in safekeeping until you return from a journey. You are already in Ang's care. All I ask is that you continue your travel and make no decisions regarding the photographs until you return. Then, I will happily restore these items to you."

"Why not just let me have them? I won't be in Katmandu until June anyway. There's no way I could do anything with them in the countryside, and by then, I'll have finished my time with Ang."

"Quite so—but, as you know, the photographs are valuable. Are you certain they will not be lost or stolen during your journey?"

Blake shot a look at Ang, who continued to stare at the floor. *Traitor! You set me up! Can't make eye contact? No wonder.*

Blake took a step forward. "So all I have to do is come back here and pick up my stuff before leaving for Katmandu and home? You'll give it all back? No questions asked?"

"That is my promise to you."

"I'd like more than your promise," Blake said. A pause followed and Ang shifted his weight uncomfortably. "I want you to write it down, like an I.O.U. And then sign it. That way, I'll know you're going to give the camera, the negatives, and the photos back. Make sure it says camera, negatives, and photos."

"As you wish." The Rinpoche spoke a few strange words to the monks. Paper and ink were brought, and soon Blake was handed a carefully lettered parchment signed by the lama.

Ang pulled Blake back to his original position. Blake shook free and glared at him.

"Ang, I want you to read this and make sure it says what it's supposed to."

Ang looked at the Rinpoche who nodded his approval. Blake passed the parchment to Ang. Finally, Ang said, "Yes. This says that when you come back, the Rinpoche will return the camera, negatives, and photographs to you. No questions asked."

"Good. Then we have a deal," Blake said as he took the I.O.U.

The lama bowed his head. Ang assumed his supplication pose and retreated with Blake.

Blake turned to exit the chamber and paused at a textile painting hung by a golden cord. In bright orange-red, the creature mih teh seemed to burst from behind a rock, displaying a jaw full of ferocious teeth and equally deadly claws. A few days ago this was a fanciful creature designed by myth. Now Blake knew yeti was real. He owned the proof. The only thing that stood in his way of revealing the truth was a trip with Ang. He could do that. He was sure of it.

Silence hung heavy in the air. Ang turned prayer wheels as they made their way out of the monastery. Back at the hut, another meal had been laid out on the low table. Blake slammed the door shut deliberately.

"Why did you take my stuff? No wonder they kicked you out of the monastery!" Blake shouted.

Seating himself at the table, Ang responded, "I was not kicked out, I simply left."

"I guess it's okay for Sherpas to steal, then!"

Ang picked up a doughy bread pocket filled with meat and took a bite. He chewed slowly. "Come and eat. Tomorrow we leave for Namche Bazaar. It is a big town and will be more what you are accustomed to."

Dropping to his knees, Blake pounded the table with his fist. "You still haven't told me why it's all right for you to steal my things!"

Ang nodded. "This is a difficult matter to explain. I apologize for taking your belongings. There are larger questions you have not yet considered."

Blake sneered. "Like what?"

"Have you thought about how these photographs might affect this whole region, my people?"

"No, not really"

"As I thought. Our journey will allow you time to think on that. In your hand, you hold the promise of the Rinpoche that all the items will be returned to you."

Blake looked at the rolled scroll he grasped tightly in his hand. The lama's promise. "The only reason I agreed to this is that I think it might be hard to keep the photographs safe while we trek around the back country. I KNOW I won't change my mind. Wait and see." A long pause followed as Blake tried to rein in his anger. Finally he said, "Why is this Rinpoche so powerful anyway? You treat him like he's a god or something." Blake picked up his meat pocket and began to eat.

"He is a very learned, wise, and respected abbot. The Rinpoche is the reincarnation of the Lama Gulo who built this monastery in 1916. As a child in Namche, he could identify items he had owned in his previous life. He was recognized as the Lama Gulo and sent to Tibet to be educated. Later, he returned to us and now is the leader of the region."

"That's like in the movie Kundun, where a kid becomes the Dalai Lama after he recognized objects he'd owned in a previous life. Slade really liked that movie."

"Who is Slade?"

"He's my best friend from back home. Once I'm home, he'll be the first to see the photos."

After the meal, Ang collected the dishes and set them outside the hut. A frosty wind swirled in, chilling the room before Ang could get the door closed. Wrapped in his sleeping bag before the fire, Blake yawned and closed his eyes.

Chapter Fifteen

The heavy stomp of yak feet and the deep calls of the herders yanked Blake from his sleep. He sat up. Shaken, he scanned the room and found Ang near the fire casting yew branches into a crackling blaze. He swayed while mumbling rhythmic chants.

Blake wriggled out of his sleeping bag and made his way over to the fire. He rubbed his arms and stamped his feet in front of the blaze, trying to get warm. Ang tossed the last bit of greenery onto the flame, and Blake stretched his hands toward the warmth.

"It became much colder during the night," Ang said.

"What time is it?" Blake asked.

"Daybreak. You heard the yaks? Some have already left for higher camps. We will have tea and proceed south."

A knock at the door prevented Blake from asking how long it would take to reach the town of Namche Bazaar. Ang hurried to the door and opened it only a crack. A teapot, cups, and small bowl were handed through, and Ang slammed the door against the frigid morning air.

Blake waited patiently for his first taste of tsampa. With a satisfied smile, Ang poured cups of tea and then added a small amount of barley flour to the mixture. He added more flour and eventually created a doughy ball. He patted his chest as if to say 'this sticks to your ribs.' Blake watched Ang slide the ball into his mouth.

Blake raised his cup, "What's in this?" A glob of something white and fatty floated freely on top of the glassy brown fluid.

"That is butter tea, which you have already had," Ang said.

Blake grabbed a handful of the powdery barley grain and smelled it. It had a rich, nutty fragrance that encouraged him to take the next step. He dumped a fistful of the flour into the tea and used one hand to try to make a ball. The flour absorbed the water quickly, forming a ball, and Blake was left with a mound of flour at the bottom of his cup.

Ang laughed good-heartedly. "You will need more tea." He poured some more hot tea into Blake's cup, and Blake completed his doughy tsampa.

Tentatively, Blake bit into the ball and chewed. "Not bad," he said. The salt and butter from the tea mixed with the flour and reminded Blake of a moist biscuit.

Packed and ready to go, Blake pulled the heavy door open far enough to squeeze out. It had snowed during the night, and several inches of snow now blanketed the valley, covering the gompa. The magical winter wonderland was marred only by the trail of the yak train headed north. The muddy brown path interrupted the quiet, untouched purity the snow had brought.

The dry snow crunched under their feet as they trudged away from Tengboche in the gray light of the morning. They came upon a thick stone gateway marking the entrance to the monastery as they descended a slight hill. Stepping inside, Blake encountered a wall of traditionally painted Buddhist designs. A pantheon of fierce deities and protectors danced around him. Directly in front of him Blake saw two huge snow lions facing each other, separated by an object suspended between them.

"Ang, what are these dogs holding?"

Ang shook his head. "Those are Snow Lions, mythical creatures holding a wish-fulfilling jewel."

"A wish fulfilling jewel? Like a Buddhist genie then?"

"What is 'genie'?"

"It's a creature that lives in a bottle and if you catch him, he has to grant you three wishes."

"No, not a genie." Ang exited the gateway while Blake lingered behind.

When Blake finally emerged, Ang was gone. The trail cut sharply right and descended. Blake hurried around the bend at a run and soon caught up to Ang. Groves of high rhododendron engulfed the path as the two travelers pushed on. Although the trees had yet to leaf, the branches were so thick with snow that it was impossible to see anything to the sides of the path. Blake coughed, feeling claustrophobic in the dark maze.

As the day grew brighter, he felt more comfortable. They left the trees behind and crossed into a rocky area cut midway up a mountain. Blake knew that to his left, the ledge dropped off a couple of hundred feet, but thankfully the path was wide enough that he didn't have to look down. Snow did not reach into this pass, at least not the last snow. *Focus straight ahead. Stay close to the mountain. And breathe, remember to breathe.*

Blake felt as if they were going to circumambulate the entire mountain. Pausing to look behind, he saw that the valley from which they had come had vanished. They had covered quite a distance in a short time, and rounding the mountain cut off the view of the monastery. Blake could just make out the warm rays from the rising sun coming over his left shoulder.

Ahead, the trail wound down into a valley. Fields lay separated into family plots that were divided by long rock walls. The brightly colored clothes of a few farmers tending their fields could be seen even at a distance.

"What are they planting? Barley?" Blake asked.

"No, these are potato fields."

As they drew near, they saw that the farmers were breaking ground and removing rocks in anticipation of the planting season. Ang waved enthusiastically, using his whole arm. The farmers returned the gesture, then went back to their labors. Farther below a group of houses with flat roofs sat together. A few dogs and children played outside, but Ang led them away from the farming village. They stopped for a quick lunch not far outside the town. Blake tore into the yak jerky and cheese with gusto.

Back on their way, the land gently rose as the trail left the valley. Sparse evergreen trees and dry brush dotted the rolling hillside. They walked a couple of miles in the shadows of Everest, Lhotse, and Ama Dablam. Cresting a knoll, they looked down into a horseshoe-shaped depression containing a town.

Ang pointed. "Namche Bazaar."

A decent-sized town at last!

The brightly colored roofs of blue, green, red, and orange sparkled in the sun, looking like a tiled mosaic. The two- and three-story flat roofed buildings, all painted white, seemed to jump out of the barren landscape with an exuberant hope.

"Let's hurry!" Blake called as he bounded in front of Ang.

Blake followed a path that dropped several levels into the terraced town. Stone walls, shoulder high, lined the path and pulled him deeper into the thriving village. The commercial success of Namche was evident with new construction everywhere. Outside, music wafted through the streets along with the clink of hammers cracking stone for new buildings. Guest lodges with brightly painted signs dotted the village. Moving toward the center of town, Blake and Ang reached the business district. First-floor shops spilled out into the streets, selling clothes, hiking gear, and virtually anything a traveler might need or want. Tibetan handicrafts and textiles sat alongside the latest in Western manufactured goods.

Blake picked up a huge decorated collar with a large brass bell and shook it. The bell clanged and he recognized the sound from the yak trains.

"Tibetan dog collar," Ang said, smirking.

"Maybe I'll get one for my dog," Blake replied.

"Americans have big dogs!"

Pushing farther on, they came to a shop selling gourmet food items. Scottish shortbread and Swiss chocolate drew Blake's eyes first. They wandered among aisles displaying French pâté, Russian sardines, and Polish sausage. Blake purchased a rainforest chocolate bar with macadamia nuts and ducked around a corner to peruse the imported Chinese foods. Some of the items he could recognize through the cellophane wrapping, but others were not visible and the Chinese labels meant nothing to him.

Back in the street, Blake ripped open the candy bar and bit off a sizable chunk. He let the flavors melt onto his tongue as he closed his eyes. This was his first reminder of home in weeks, and he remembered the first time Slade had given him one of these rainforest bars. It tasted even better here.

Ang opened a bottle of chang and took a long swig. The two walked by more textiles and jewelry and paused at the end of the street near a guest lodge.

"I have stayed here before. The rates are as fair as anywhere, and the food is good," Ang said.

The large dining room rang out with laughter as they made their way to a table. At this time of day, most of the trekkers had returned from their excursions and the room was full of joyous and hungry travelers. They took seats at one of the several large wooden tables, squeezed up against a wall. Barley beer flowed freely and many travelers engaged in animated conversation while downing large quantities of food being served family style.

A small, brightly dressed Sherpa girl served them. She smiled and asked Ang something. Soon Tibetan tea and plates arrived. Bowls of rice, steaming vegetables, and savory meats circulated almost continuously around the table.

Blake held one of the bowls and peered in, "Yak?"

Ang nodded. Blake took a large helping. As he mixed some vegetables into the rice, he realized this would be the first time he'd had fresh vegetables in days. Dad wouldn't approve of the food he'd had on the trail, but then what did Dad care? His only concern had been to get rid of him.

"Are you going to drink your tea?" Ang asked.

"No, I don't like it."

Ang took the cup while he motioned to the serving girl. She came over and asked Blake something. Their eyes met. She was pretty, with soft brown eyes and a dainty smile. He wished he could talk to her. Ang said something, and she disappeared. *Great going, Ang!* His disappointment didn't last, because the girl quickly returned with a bottle of soda. She put it down nervously and left the room. Ang started a conversation with another Sherpa off to his left while Blake shoveled food in as fast as he could. As he chewed, he scanned the room looking for the girl. She remained busy bringing in new bowls and removing plates. During the entire meal, their eyes never met again.

After eating, Blake followed Ang up to the top floor where they found their room. They dropped their packs, and Blake sprawled out on one of the two beds, yawning.

"I need a nap. Maybe we can explore more of the town tonight?"

"You rest. I will come back for you in a few hours," Ang said.

"Okay." *Where's he going now? Isn't he as tired as I am?*

Ang closed the door behind him and Blake sprang to the window. Watching the exit, Blake saw Ang emerge and cross the street. He joined several other Sherpa men sitting on a bench smoking cigarettes.

Blake stretched his arms to the ceiling feeling his tired muscles strain. He ran his thumb around his jeans, realizing he had lost weight. He would never have thought trekking so strenuous. Untying the laces of his boots, he struggled to wrestle his feet free. His foot continued to heal, well protected under the bandage. He lay back and fell into a deep sleep.

Ang returned a few hours late, as promised, and shook Blake out of a dream, saying, "Up, up! Time to go!"

Blake dropped his legs over the side of the bed and pulled himself up into a sitting position. The sun had receded, leaving him in gray shadows. Ang snapped on a table lamp and the bright light made Blake recoil.

"Come. Come!" Ang continued.

"Where are we going?" Blake asked, rolling his head and stretching.

"Tea house, just up the street."

Blake forced his feet into his boots and, leaving them untied, he rose and followed Ang out into the night. Even busier than before, the street buzzed with activity. Tourists packed the small shops and Sherpas crowded together in groups talking. A happy and festive mood permeated the crowd. They wove in and out of the throng as they made their way to the tea house, passing under colorful prayer flags swaying gently.

The tea house, a new single-story structure, blared Chinese music into the street. Ang pushed his way past the crowd at the door. Blake followed and stepped into the establishment, assaulted by heavy smoke and dim light. To the left, a long bar was packed with patrons. Tables, chairs, and people filled the place, and everyone screamed to be heard over the music. Blake glanced back toward the bar and recognized someone.

Brian, sitting down, was not as imposing as the first time Blake had laid eyes on him. His hair stood on end, and Blake wondered if he owned a comb. Ang found a seat at a table with the Sherpa friends Blake had seen him with earlier. Blake left Ang and moved toward the bar. Brian noticed him approach and jumped to his feet. Dwarfed next to Brian, Blake pushed his shoulders up while Brian slapped him hard on the back.

"Hey, Blake! Good to see you," Brian yelled.

Blake swam in the pungent scent of Brian's beer breath and he noticed that Brian's eyes were glassy and wild.

"What are you doing here?" Blake screamed over the noise.

Slamming a bottle of chang down on the bar, Brian shouted defensively, "Hey, I'm just having a good time!"

"I know that, but why aren't you climbing?"

His body became rigid as he spat, "I guess I've seen enough dead bodies this year. What's your excuse?"

Blake took a step back, fearful. "I gotta go. Ang's waiting for me." He turned and fought the crowd to get back to Ang.

No one noticed Blake slide onto the bench near his friend because they were so involved in their own conversations. The smoke from cigarettes hung over the tables like smog over cities. Blake coughed into his hand, and as he looked up, he saw her across the room. With her back against the wall, the serving girl from the lodge sipped tea. Her silver earrings sparkled when she turned her head toward the room's fireplace. Blake considered his options. He could stay with Ang and listen to the singsong conversation he couldn't decipher or he could go and try to talk to this girl.

Rubbing his hands nervously, he finally pulled himself off the bench. *What do I have to lose?* He cut a path around the other patrons and arrived at her side. A moment of recognition passed as their eyes met. Blake smiled, unsure what to say. He knew no Sherpa.

"Hi. I'm staying at the lodge where you work." Blake hoped she knew some English.

"Yes, thank you," she nodded.

Did she understand me or is that all the English she knows? Let's find out.

"I'm Blake. What is your name?"

"Mingma," she said.

A shove from behind pushed Blake away from Mingma. A stocky young Sherpa man came forward, shouting. He pushed Blake against the wall, further separating him from Mingma. Sour breath spit angry words. Blake didn't understand what was wrong. *Is this her boyfriend, her brother...? Did I do something wrong just by talking to her?*

Blake ducked a punch as the man's rage only seemed to grow. His hands raised in defense, Blake stepped away from the wall, trying to defuse the situation. "Look, I'm sorry. I don't want to fight." *This guy is smaller than me, but he's tough. I can't fight him.* Another punch grazed Blake's chin as the man closed the distance between them.

Blake started backing up. The crash of benches overturning didn't distract him from the advancing Sherpa. The crowd pulled away from the confrontation, making room for the fight to continue. Blake headed for the door but found his exit blocked by spectators. The Sherpa yelled some more and ran forward, hands raised.

Ang exploded onto the floor, placing himself in front of Blake. The man continued to advance and swung punches at Ang, who countered every move. Then the situation erupted into a full-scale bar fight as others from the crowd jumped in against Ang. Immediately, Ang's friends joined in to support him. The majority of the local patrons threw themselves into the fray on one side or the other while many of the tourists made for the door. Pushed and shoved toward the back of the room, Blake managed to stay out of the action. Chairs crashed, beer bottles flew, and mayhem reigned.

Blake heard the cry of tin being ripped back from above him. From a gaping hole in the ceiling, Brian screamed, "Here, kid!" Lying prone on the roof, Brian threw a rope down.

"Tie it under your arms, quick!"

Blake did as commanded, and Brian pulled him up onto the roof to safety. "Thanks!" Blake said. Together they replaced the metal sheet.

Brian moved higher on the roof and sat down. He pulled a bottle of chang out from his coat. Shaking his head, he said. "Damn, kid, you sure know how to get into trouble."

"It wasn't my fault. I only said a couple of words to her before her boyfriend showed up."

Beer trickled down Brian's chin. "Advice to the inexperienced, women will always get you into trouble. Especially here. Hell of a good fight, though," he smirked.

MAGIC AND ENLIGHTENMENT

Chapter Sixteen

Blake found Ang back at the lodge tending a black eye. Standing before a full-sized, cracked mirror he gently pressed the surrounding skin and winced in pain. Blake's image appeared in the mirror, contrasting sharply with the older, smaller Sherpa.

Turning around Ang said, "I looked for you after and could not find you."

"Brian rescued me in the middle of it all. He pulled me onto the roof with some climbing gear."

Ang raised an eyebrow but said nothing. He looked him up and down and finally asked, "So, you are not injured?"

Blake shook his head as he peeled off his coat. He sat on the bed and tugged at his boots. "You know, I tried talking to her boyfriend, but he just didn't understand. He kept getting madder and madder. I mean, I wasn't even doing anything. I didn't want to fight him."

"Too much beer and too much jealousy. Sometimes, it makes an explosion."

"Then you jumped in and the guy's friends jumped in! It got crazy."

"I know," Ang answered quietly. "In a few months, you will go home. Then you will find a girl. It is hard, I know this. Sometimes, I see pretty girls too."

"You? You're married." Blake chuckled, nervously.

"Yes. Still, one sometimes sees a woman and there is an attraction."

Is this where he gives me the birds and bees lecture following Sherpa tradition? He vividly remembered the time several years before when his father sat him down with some old medical texts. It had all been very clinical and very detached, not really embarrassing, but not really informative either. He knew the facts. The facts were easy. The hard stuff was the emotional part. How do you ask a girl out? What if she says no? What if she says yes? How do you know when a girl likes you back? What is love? How do you know it will last? Does it last? Is it supposed to last? His mom and dad's didn't. Dad saw to that. If only things had stayed the same. Maybe love is a fantasy.

"I will share a technique from my days at gompa that will serve you while you are here. When you see a pretty girl and you get that feeling, you must imagine her as a corpse. You must see her dead on the ground decaying, her gray hair falling out. Her skin bloated, bruised, and cracking. Puddles of fluid leaking from the body. Flies..."

"Okay," Blake said interrupting. "I get it!"

"The more vivid you make the image; the faster your attraction will be extinguished."

A week passed in Namche. Blake wandered the streets during the day visiting the shops, trying some of the international delicacies using his pocket money. He collected post cards to show Slade and snapped photos of the town. Every day felt like a festival, awash in the cultural mix of the tourists and the locals.

Every once in a while, he'd come across someone who spoke English. Soon the conversation would turn to sharing where he came from. He always said California, never mentioning Ohio. He didn't want to betray his mother and her life, but he still felt connected to Los Angeles. And besides, everyone knew LA. No one would recognize the small town he lived in now.

The immediate connection he sensed whenever he met another American seemed odd, but somehow meeting an American here automatically made them the same. Back home, he wouldn't have found anything in common with the trekkers and climbers that he had met, but here they were Americans in a faraway place. Boundaries evaporated and similarities became more important than the differences. Before he left home, he had concerns about traveling alone, especially with the threat of terrorism abroad after 9/11. He had decided not to tell people he was an American or flaunt his roots. It seemed best to lie low. But whenever he heard English, he hoped he had found another American. Blake also met Canadians and people from the UK. He felt connected to them too, but not so intensely. Speaking the same language made them able to communicate, but their experiences separated them.

Upon returning from his afternoon foray, Blake found Ang sitting on the floor in their lodge reading a newspaper. Ang now spent his evenings scanning newspapers and reading old magazines he'd found, instead of frequenting the bars and tea shops.

Ang looked up from the paper and said, "Good, you are back early. I want to show you where we will go tomorrow." The paper fell to the floor, and Ang rose and retrieved a map from his pack. He smoothed the ancient-looking trekking guide out on the bed.

"We are here and we will follow the river to this village," he said as he ran his finger over the route.

Looking over Ang's shoulder, Blake asked, "What's in Thame?"

"It is a traditional Sherpa village. Old, small and quiet, not like Namche."

"Maybe we should just head to Katmandu and spend a month or so there. There's more to do in the city, and I could contact my Mom and get her to wire more money."

Ang shook his head. "We do not need more money. We go to Thame. Perhaps you have forgotten the promise you made to the Rinpoche. You no longer want your camera returned?"

"Oh, I want it back all right! I just don't want to spend all my time in this country in ancient villages that time forgot," Blake said with his hands on his hips.

Ang moved forward, so close Blake could feel his breath on his chin. "I made a promise to the Rinpoche and to your father. We will leave for Thame in the morning." Without raising his voice, Ang made it clear to Blake that he could enforce his wishes.

The next morning Blake raised the window shade and grunted. A steel-colored mist hung over Namche. They would walk in the clouds on their travel west.

Ang secured the rest of his belongings and bent to lift the heavy pack onto his back. Ignoring him, Blake popped his headphones on to block out any possibility of conversation along the trail.

The town slept as they stepped into the empty street and made their way past the closed shops. Prayer flags whipped in the light breeze. Blake pulled himself deeper into his jacket and retreated into the familiar sounds of a Goth band.

The level path was well traveled, and walking was easy. The few days in Namche had allowed Blake's wounded foot to heal almost completely, and his leg muscles felt as good as new. Even after they had been on the trail for an hour, the sun had not burned its way through the mist. It made the journey somber and did nothing to lift Blake's spirits. During the night he had thought about breaking out on his own and traveling to Katmandu without Ang. To hell with Dad's plan. He could make his own plan. But then, as his idea took shape, he realized a few things. Traveling alone could be dangerous. He didn't know the area, the trails, or the people. The fantasy of being on his own and showing Ang and his dad he could survive alone occupied him for a while, but he finally grasped the personal cost of that choice. Leaving Ang would mean he had forfeited the camera and photos, and he couldn't do that. He had to stick it out. He made that promise and he would keep it.

The Bhote Kosi River carved its way east from Thame, and Ang and Blake followed its course. Blake marveled at the deep, crystal-blue stream and how it contrasted against the dry, barren ridges they crossed. The region flaunted opposites. Clear, sunny days shattered by sudden violent storms. The world's tallest, icy peaks surrounded by low, green meadows. Ang in his world and he out of place in it.

Stone fences enclosed potato plots on the edges of Thame. As they drew closer, Sherpas could be seen working in the fields. Blake sighed and removed his headset. *Another tiny village in the middle of nowhere.* Traditional-mud walled houses sprang into sight as they walked on. Simple structures painted white marked the agricultural village. Blake guessed the population of the town was probably less than fifty, judging by the number of houses.

He and Ang circumvented the potato fields and entered the village, exchanging friendly waves all along the way. Outside the first dwelling, they came upon a diminutive old woman stacking dried yak droppings near a doorway. She turned to face the newcomers and flashed a toothless grin.

"Nyima," Ang called out.

The woman came closer, and Blake realized she stood only four and a half feet tall. Oddly, her arms and legs seemed frail and spindly, barely able to support her. A large head sat on top of the tiny body, disproportionate to the rest of her, and large, almond-shaped eyes met Blake's. He looked at the ground, trying not to stare.

"Ang Thondup!" she cried. She hurried to him while a string of Sherpa words flowed like the river they had just left.

Blake stood to the side while the two reacquainted themselves. Subconsciously, he allowed his shoulders to slump as he wondered what birth defect had affected this old woman. Ang introduced Blake, and Nyima ushered them both inside her home and before a smoky fire.

They sat cross-legged at a low table. A plush rug kept them comfortable on the compressed dirt floor. Nyima fussed about and eventually bought the familiar Tibetan tea. Ang smiled appreciatively while Blake groaned mentally. *What I'd give for a soda or even a regular cup of tea!*

"Blake is growing fond of our tea, Nyima," Ang said in Tibetan and then translated it for Blake. He poked Blake in the shoulder.

Blake nodded to the old woman and forced a smile.

"Nyima has said that the rest of her family is out in the potato field behind the village. After tea, we will go see if we can help," Ang said.

A short walk behind Nyima's house brought them to the family's walled in plot. A couple and two boys held hoes breaking up the soil in preparation for planting. Ang took the woman's hoe, and Blake relieved the youngest boy. The woman and boy returned to the house. Ang and the man worked side by side, talking to each other. Blake smashed at the soil while watching the older boy in his peripheral vision. When the boy came across a rock, he bent and threw it toward the nearest wall. Blake put his rocks in a pile and waited to throw them until he was ready to move to another section. Soon the boy copied Blake's system.

Physical labor at altitude quickly had Blake sweating in his hiking gear. He unzipped his jacket and stuffed his hat and gloves in his pockets. The sun finally melted its way through the clouds. The sun, along with the work, felt good. Good until the pads of his hands started to hurt. He shifted the hoe to his left hand and rubbed the skin just below the fingers. The boy came over to look, and without words, he showed Blake his right hand with the thick calluses of a farmer. Taking Blake by the arm, he led him to the stone fence to sit.

A few minutes later with the work on the field accomplished, Ang motioned for Blake to come. The four trudged back to the house.

In the evening, the Sherpa family gathered around the table, sharing a stew of yak meat and potatoes. Blake dunked a wad of unleavened potato bread into the savory mixture and followed it with hefty swig of tea. The talk was low and polite, but because it was in Sherpa, it was impossible for Blake to understand.

During a lull in the conversation, Ang asked, "Nyima, will you share the tale of your land? Blake does not know of it. I shall translate your words."

Nyima smiled and rolled her eyes. Blake realized she must have told the tale countless times to family and strangers alike, but she probably never grew tired of it. Ang's request meant that he enjoyed her stories.

"I was born seventy-three years ago in the Baian-Kara-Ula Mountains that lie between China and Tibet. My family farmed barley on a small plot, and like everyone else we were poor. Some years were better than others, but we never starved. I had three sisters and many cousins!" Ang translated for Blake.

"But you want to know about the time before that. Our history. How we are different from the Sherpas." Nyima grasped her son-in-law's face and playfully shook it. She continued. "I am Dzopa!" She slapped the table. "They are Dzopa also," she said, pointing to her two grandsons.

"Our ancestors came to this place from a faraway planet in the Sirius star system. On two occasions my ancestors came to explore. Twenty thousand years ago they scouted the region to see if life could be maintained here. Then in 1014 C. E., they returned. Bad luck followed them, and their conveyance crashed." Nyima sipped her tea while Ang spoke in English.

Blake's jaw hung loose as he held his cup pressed firmly to his bottom lip. *Yeti and aliens! She's a little alien grandma! Weeks ago, I would have written her off as a lunatic, but now? How can I? But this can't be true! Just because she looks weird doesn't prove she's an alien. Right?*

Nyima set her cup down and resumed the tale. "The local people were fierce warriors on horseback. They hunted down and killed many of the star visitors. Those who survived hid in caves. Eventually, the local people saw that the visitors were not a threat, and peace filled the mountains. The locals and the star people intermarried, and a new people, like me, came to be." She paused and looked deep into Blake's eyes, making him uncomfortable. Averting her glance, Blake scratched at the remnants of black nail polish lining his cuticles.

Okay, she's not a 'pure' alien—she's a hybrid. That makes it so much easier and so much more believable!

Ang coaxed the rest of the story by asking, "What happened when you were young?"

"Ah, yes. The village was honored by a visit from a Chinese professor interested in the caves. None of us had ever been in the caves. Children were forbidden to go near them. Even adults stayed away. How odd this scientist wanted to explore there!"

"What did he find?" Blake asked.

"Cave paintings lined the walls, showing the sun, the moon, and the stars, and there were crude images of beings with over-sized heads. I saw them along with the graves. When the graves were opened, the professor found the skeletons of the little people with the big skulls. Later, hundreds of stone discs were removed and taken back to China. We all knew that the graves were of our ancestors and the stone discs were a record of our early time on this planet." Nyingma smiled demurely, having made her point.

Blake looked to Ang for guidance. "Thank you for telling Blake about your people."

Outside under the stars, Blake shivered in the cold, clear night. Ang lit a cigarette and inhaled it deeply.

"Is there any truth to her story? Do you believe it?" Blake questioned.

"Perhaps," Ang said, looking up at the glittering stars.

Chapter Seventeen

Blake woke to find himself alone in the smoky half-light of the morning. Outside he heard the laughter and running feet of children. He stretched and eased his boots on. He pulled back a heavy curtain and looked out into the yard. Half a dozen young children had gathered to play. The family's sons were not there, and neither was the rest of the family. *And where has Ang gone?*

Nyima came through the front door with the day's supply of yak dung. She placed the bundle near the fire and then turned her attention to cooking breakfast. Blake darted outside, relieved that she hadn't spoken to him.

Blake saw Ang coming back from the potato field. The children had gathered stones and constructed a platform in the yard. One child sat atop a makeshift throne while the others gathered before him. One by one, the children prostrated themselves in front of the boy on the throne. Each child stepped forward and, with great dignity, unwrapped a winter scarf from around his or her neck and handed it to the boy on the raised platform. The boy took each scarf, said something, and returned it to its owner.

Ang shot a sideways glance at the children playing as he approached Blake.

"What are they doing?" Blake asked.

"They are taking turns being a lama. Perhaps one of them will have that honor someday."

"Probably not the girls," Blake shot back.

"In this lifetime, the girls could choose to attend a nunnery." Ang lowered the hoe he'd been carrying to the ground.

"And in other lifetimes? Can the girls be lamas in future lives?" Blake asked.

Ang took a seat on the stone wall and indicated that Blake should also sit. "Where to begin? The simple answer to your question is that the girls could come back as boys in a future life and chose to go to monastery. And the boys could return as girls. Or perhaps they will stay the same gender for eons."

"Don't Buddhists also believe that someone can return as an animal?" Blake asked.

"Yes, but you are getting ahead of my explanation. In order for me to explain all this, I must put it into the proper context. Let me tell you some of the things we believe about this life."

"But Ang, I just want to know about reincarnation," Blake said.

"Patience, please! We will be together for many weeks. Allow me this small indulgence."

Blake propped his elbow on his knee and rested his chin in his hand. "All right. Go on, put it in context."

Ang beamed with delight. "We believe in The Four Noble Truths taught by Shakumuni Buddha. Buddha looked at man's suffering like a doctor examining a patient. The symptoms were noted, a diagnosis made, and ultimately a prognosis given. You will be able to relate to this, being a doctor's son."

"Hmm, I suppose," Blake said.

Ang raised his index finger. "First is the Truth of Suffering. Here we examine symptoms. Our unenlightened lives are full of suffering that can take many forms. I am certain you have known physical and emotional suffering in this life." Blake nodded. "That is one kind of suffering. Another kind concerns the suffering due to change. For example, perhaps you would like to have a new car. You work hard to buy the car, and for a short time, you are happy with it. Then, over time, the car rusts, it begins to make funny sounds, and soon it will not run at all. The car no longer makes you happy, and you suffer because the car has changed."

"But everyone knows when they buy a car, it won't last forever. I'd just buy another one," Blake interjected.

"That is correct. However, it is the nature of everything to change. What makes you happy today will not make you happy when it changes. You take pride in your friendship with Slade, but what will happen when Slade goes off to college and finds new friends?"

"Okay, well, I can see that change might make you unhappy, but can't change ever be a good thing?"

"It might appear so. Perhaps you will meet a special girl on your flight back to the United States. You have met a new person and this makes you happy. However, in the long term, all relationships are temporary. She may meet another boy, or circumstances may draw her away from you. Even if the relationship survives for a human lifetime, she will one day die. Then your misery would be extreme."

Blake folded his hands. "I suppose that's right, but it's a pretty pessimistic philosophy on life."

"Not at all," Ang continued. "I will show you how Buddha was actually very optimistic. But first, more on suffering. The final kind of suffering comes about as a result of your past lives. Negative actions in previous lives rebound to this life. Some suffering we experience today is the consequence of past actions."

"Terrific! So that means I'm suffering now for something I did in the past that I don't even remember. That doesn't seem fair to me."

"Have you never suffered the consequences of something you did, even after some time had passed?"

"Yeah, I guess so. When I was little, I took a screwdriver and scratched my name on my dad's new car. He didn't find it for a week or so because he was on a trip. But I got in real trouble when he came home."

"A human lifetime is small in comparison to all our existences, and our past actions are dealt with eventually. Now we must talk about the Truth of the Origin of Suffering. This is the diagnosis part. Shakyamuni taught that suffering comes from desire. You have probably guessed there are different kinds of desire. What does desire mean to you?"

Blake pondered the question. "Desire is about want. I want something."

"That is correct. That would be the desire for pleasure and it could take many forms, depending on the individual. It could be a new car, a new house, a certain job, a certain woman. Another kind of desire comes from wanting to live forever. This we call desire for continued existence. You have probably met someone who lives like they will live forever and gives no thought to their own mortality." Blake frowned and nodded. "The last kind of desire involves the desire for nonexistence. If death is the end of everything and is inevitable, then no one should find happiness in the present life. All these desires are mistaken and based on ignorance. Lasting happiness is possible. That is the prognosis and it is very optimistic. Buddha brought the good news that we can all achieve this."

"Only if we stop wanting all this stuff?" Blake said.

"Precisely. We must remove the cause of our suffering—desire. As people, we have false ideas about what is worthwhile, pleasurable, or desirable. In the unenlightened state, we exist in ignorance or perhaps a better way of saying it is we have many misperceptions. This series of mistaken views leads us to display disturbing emotions and engage in negative behaviors. Things like greed, pride, hatred, and jealousy. The Noble Eightfold Path helps us deal with all that. It is through practice we begin to overcome mistaken perceptions and glimpse ultimate reality."

"Does all this come from your monastery days?"

"It does, but all Sherpas know these things."

"All right, what is the Noble Eightfold Path?"

"That will have to wait for another time. Look!" Ang exclaimed and pointed down the path.

A row of horses made its way toward them, kicking up a dust cloud that hung near the ground as they approached from the opposite side of the village. The group moved as if floating, passing farmhouses and youngsters who came out to wave. Their fanciful costumes undulated with the motion of the horses. Waves of bright colors danced on the horizon and then drew close enough for Ang and Blake to make out faces.

A middle aged man, mounted on the lead horse, raised a hand in greeting. Ang stood up and said to Blake, "It is a wedding party taking the bride to the groom's village." Dressed in their finest attire, the group rode until the bride, crying, reached them. She wiped her eyes with a cloth and seemed oblivious to their presence.

Blake stood near Ang and said, "Tears of joy?"

"Perhaps. However, she is leaving the only home she has ever known, and she may not ever have met the groom."

The last two horses moved through carrying two women talking quietly. Ang sat back down.

"Was your marriage arranged too?"

"No, I met my wife when we both were carrying supplies into the mountains."

Nyima appeared at the door and called to them. From behind the house emerged the family, ready for breakfast.

"You'll tell me more about the noble fold thing later? You won't just leave me suffering, right?" Blake laughed.

"We will have time for all this. Let us eat now."

The family gathered around the table, taking their usual positions. Ang and Blake squeezed in, sitting side by side across from Nyima. Boiled potatoes and dried yak were served along with the all-too-familiar butter tea. With a strong appetite, stimulated by the mountain air and the work from the previous day, Blake tore into the meal.

"Nyima, with such good food, we must have a good tale. Perhaps you could tell of the Lha?" Ang said, savoring the hot butter tea. The two grandsons nodded in approval. "Blake, I shall translate for you."

Nyima chewed her potatoes, taking a moment to gather her thoughts. Then, with great abandon, she launched into the story, and Ang translated.

"A long time ago, our planet was empty of all we know today. Then it was called Dzambu Lying. The Lha people came and settled. They were a great people with great powers. Using their minds, they created food and tools, transforming the planet and living comfortably. Their profound ability to meditate made them glow with inner radiance."

Blake wrestled with a piece of jerky while the little grandmother continued her story.

"Our ancient scriptures tell us these people were our ancestors. They made use of local plants, and one of those hurt the people. Over time, the Lha lost their abilities and they became human." Nyima smiled as she finished talking.

"Okay, so this was way before the Dzopa, right?" Blake asked.

"Correct."

Blake wiped his hands on his jeans. "Well, no doubt George Lucas could do something with this."

The family returned to talking quietly amongst themselves while Blake looked at Ang. *Why does he keep bringing up these weird stories? It's getting really hard to know what is real and what isn't. It's hard enough dealing with the fact that the yeti is real, and now I'm having to question everything. Maybe Nyima's stories are just fables, or maybe there is an element that has some truth. How am I supposed to know what to think?*

Later that afternoon, Ang introduced Blake to potato farming. Ang demonstrated the proper method of cutting the tubers that would go into the ground while the family prepared the beds for planting. Each cutting had to have at least one eye to produce a plant successfully. Blake sliced potatoes and laid the sections out on a mesh cloth to dry. As he cut hundreds of potatoes, he wondered if he'd see them in his sleep. Of course, dreaming of potatoes might be a relief if the other alternative meant dreaming about the Lha people. And then, as he remembered the Dzopa, an even more horrifying possibility came to mind. The fuel for his dreams could be an alien race hunted down and slaughtered by men on horseback. He forced the images out of his head, determined to concentrate on planting potatoes. Holding a large potato before putting it to the knife, Blake reveled in the fact that he could hold this vegetable. He felt its weight, and when he lifted it to his nose, he smelled the pungent aroma of soil and knew it contained life. It would keep this Sherpa family alive in one of the most remote and desolate places on earth. The potato was real.

Blake cut and planted more potatoes over the next week than he thought he'd consumed in his entire life, including the bags of chips he'd knocked off with Slade. He worked quickly now, falling into a rhythm born of practice. With the skin on his hands dried and cracked, he learned to smear yak fat on them. Dirt gathered under the fingernails that back home often sported black or green nail polish. At night, he tried to dig out some of the grime with a length of straw, but it never fully worked.

Nyima promised to make their last night with the family special. Blake wondered and worried all day about what she meant by that. Enough stories had been told and enough work had been done. He wished that he and Ang could just slip off unnoticed.

Everyone finished in the fields and returned to the house. A thick aroma of juniper incense assaulted Blake's nostrils as he stepped over the threshold. In the far corner of the room, on her knees, Nyima beckoned them to join her. Everyone gathered at the family shrine, dutifully obeying the tiny grandmother.

On a small table stood a golden statue of Buddha surrounded by seven offering bowls, illuminated by many butter lamps. A copper plate supporting a long-stemmed vessel containing black tea was the daily offering to the god Mahakala. Off to one side, a framed photograph of a smiling lama completed the altar.

The family, along with Ang and Blake, knelt down, and Nyima began her prayers. Ang translated.

"We will offer prayers of thanks and well-being for the good company we have had and for their further travels in safety." Around him, Blake heard the family chant mantras with Nyima. Ang joined in, highlighting Blake's separateness.

Chapter Eighteen

"But why are we going to another monastery? Why couldn't we stay in Namche or head to Katmandu?" Blake asked as they trudged away from the village of Thame. Behind them, the family stood near the doorway waving their goodbyes.

"I must fulfill my promise to the Rinpoche. Going to a city would not suit our purpose," Ang said.

Blake threw his hands into the air. "And what is 'our purpose'?"

"Knowledge is our purpose. You must gain this to make decisions regarding the camera and photographs."

"I told you, I know what my decision will be. I'm only going along with this to get my stuff back and meet my father in Katmandu. Then it's back to the States and hello CNN."

During the time they had spent with the family, the gompa had been visible from the potato plot. The monastery appeared embedded like a diamond in a fine setting. It sat perched on a high ridgeline before them. They heard the thunderous sound of water tumultuously rushing and crashing as they drew closer. The incline of the trail steepened, and the backs of Blake's calves strained to respond to the challenge. The path disappeared, cutting left behind stunted shrubbery. Rounding the corner, Blake gasped. Timber planks cut a ladder of stairs into the mountain rising nearly three stories straight up.

Anxiety showed in Blake's voice. "You've got to be kidding!"

Ang surveyed the situation. "It is not terribly difficult. I will tie you with climbing gear."

Blake stood with hands on hips, looking straight up. He had only climbed those rock walls at the mall back home and, in comparison, that was easy. Ang withdrew a length of rope and some hooks. He secured Blake, running the rope under his arms and across his chest with the skill of an expert. With the other end, Ang lashed the two of them together.

"I will go first. It is just like climbing any other ladder. Go slowly and do not look down. The rope is only a precaution," Ang said. Blake nodded and retreated to the mental dialogue that always took over when fear occurred with time to think.

Ang's a climber, an expert climber. This is nothing. Even at the top, it's only like being on a high roof. I can do this. I hope I can do this. What if I get partway up and panic? That won't happen. It's only three stories. Ferris wheels are higher than this. I remember when I was four, being caught at the top of one of those. But that was with Mom, and I don't even think I was scared.

Together they moved toward the ladder. Ang stepped onto the first board and reached for the next timber. Blake waited for Ang to signal when to start climbing. The rope allowed Ang to reach the eighth step before stopping to look down.

"All right, Blake! Come slowly. Do not look down."

Blake began climbing. First one foot, then the other. He stood on the first rail. *All I have to do is repeat this until I get to the top. Piece of cake!* He scaled the first half of the ladder and, looking up, he saw that Ang was near the top. Lifting his right foot to the next step, Blake dislodged a rock that rolled over his foot and plummeted over the edge, bouncing off timbers, hurtling its way to the ground. He watched as the rock smashed pieces of wood and sent flying debris careening downward, and then it struck him that he was looking down. Now, fully aware of being precariously perched on a mountainside, Blake froze. The line tethering them stretched taut as Ang proceeded to climb. The sudden tightness of the rope stopped Ang cold.

"No, not down! Blake, look up here—now!"

The order jerked Blake's attention away from the mini-avalanche, and he gazed up at Ang.

Calmly, Ang commanded, "Climb up two steps, and I will wait."

Inside his gloves, Blake's fingers ached, clutching at a timber. Sweat broke out along his brow, and perspiration ran down his cheek. His breathing became shallow as he tried to dislodge a hand and move forward. Fear held his body rigid on the ladder. Closing his eyes and swallowing hard, he tried again. *Impossible! I can't move.*

Above him, Ang called, "Blake, can you climb?"

Fully gripped in the terror, Blake could not force himself to speak. He couldn't even answer Ang. He shook his head awkwardly while looking straight ahead into the red-brown hillside. Within seconds, Ang appeared at his side, supported by the same wooden rail. He uncurled Blake's hand and moved it to the next timber. He lifted Blake's leg and pushed it up. Feeling his body move, Blake responded and began to gain control. The spell was broken and he reached for the next step on his own as Ang fell in behind. Finally, Blake breeched the top and stepped clear of the ladder. Ang pulled himself up and led them away from the edge before unhooking the gear.

"Sorry," Blake said staring at the ground.

"It is all right. You are not a climber, and even climbers can have difficulties. Perhaps I will tell you the story of the tough Australian Air Force pilot who soiled his pants." Ang flashed a grin in remembrance and patted Blake on the shoulder.

The path circled to the left at a slight incline. The sound of rushing water assaulted them as they neared the gompa. Sitting on a ridge, facing north, the monastery clung to the mountainside, framed by a steep waterfall on one side. It sat as if created for a fairy tale long ago, partially obscured by stunted trees and the mist from the water. Not far from the base of the waterfall, a gigantic wooden prayer wheel spun continuously in the ceaseless flow of the river, sending out prayers for the benefit of all.

Far simpler than Tengboche, Thame's Monastery was a single-story building with only one entrance. Ang and Blake approached, and a solitary peacock emerged from under a bush and spread its tail wide, displaying its iridescent blue and green plumage. The bird casually strolled in front of them as if announcing their arrival at some exotic palace. Blake shook his head but said nothing. They followed, and the peacock settled itself near the base of the stairs, watching the travelers.

Mounting the stairs, they saw a carved wooden door, framed in red with a huge brass knocker. Ang rapped loudly, disturbing the peacock, which fled back to its place under the bush. Several moments passed, and Ang was about to knock again when the door flew open. A tall monk draped in crimson, with shaved head, stood to the side to let them in.

Ang spoke a few words, and the monk nodded. He led them inside and left them standing in the dark entryway, which was quiet, almost to the point of being eerie. Blake felt the effects of incense on his lungs before he smelled it. The sounds of rhythmic chanting emanated from deep within the gompa.

Leaning toward Ang, Blake asked in a whisper, "Are we going to stay here tonight?"

"Yes, several nights probably. First we must meet the abbot."

The wall closest to Ang opened, becoming a door and revealing a small room. An old man, bent with age, pushed through, rattling his prayer beads, wood against wood. His eyes twinkled in the flame cast by butter lamps that lit the tiny space.

"We shall speak English! I have been wanting to practice and now I have the chance," he said as he took Blake by the hand. "I have been expecting you. The Rinpoche and I are fine friends. Is 'fine' the correct word?" He looked expectantly at Blake.

"I suppose so."

"Wonderful! You will stay many days and I will practice my English!"

He led Blake back into his chamber without even acknowledging Ang. The light of the flickering lamps danced off the walls momentarily illuminating ornate fabric paintings of bodhisattvas and deities. Along one wall, ancient looking texts neatly lined shelves. A dozen brightly colored canaries flitted about a large bamboo cage. The abbot gestured for Blake and Ang to sit, and he took his position atop a slightly raised dais. Stepping off a wire perch, a white Macaw hopped onto the man's rounded shoulder. The abbot chuckled and whispered a few words to his avian companion.

"Ang, it has been many years since I have seen you. The last time was in Delhi at festival. How is your family?" the abbot asked.

"They are well. Thank you."

The macaw took the old man's earlobe into his beak and chewed. The abbot nodded, whipping his ear free, and continued, "As I have stated, I have been expecting you both. The Rinpoche has told me that you and Blake are working on an important project. The nature of the work has to do with Blake's education, I am led to believe. That is where we, at Thame, can be useful. The Rinpoche has assured me that you are to have full access to the gompa and all our work here. We do not usually entertain guests in this way, but I know you both are setting about an important task."

The macaw jumped to the abbot's head, breaking the severity of the moment and causing Blake to laugh. Nonplussed, the aged lama raised a hand and placed the naughty bird back on his stand.

"Blake, please come to me any time you have questions. It is our aim to make your stay comfortable and...educational." He rose, indicating the meeting was over.

Blake and Ang stood and started backing up. Halting suddenly, Blake stopped and walked forward. "I do have a question. Do you have a phone here?"

"No. We are too remote for such things," the abbot answered patiently.

"Then how did the Rinpoche tell you about us?"

The old man stroked his white bird. "Ah. He appeared in a dream telling me of your mission and my part in it."

"In a dream?"

"Yes. I have also seen some of your travels and things that have not yet happened."

"Really? Like what?"

The abbot considered the challenge. Slowly he said, "The view of a cold, starry night on a metal rooftop. You with a friend."

The truth of the lama's words hit Blake like a well-placed punch. He reeled back, understanding that not even Ang knew all those details. "What else?" Blake pleaded.

"It is not for me to reveal your future."

"Is it bad? You can tell me, I can take it."

"Good, bad—all matters of perception. Something your education will no doubt address. Please excuse me while I tend to my birds."

The abbot pulled a bag of seeds from under his robe and the bamboo cage erupted with activity and wild chirping. Another younger monk poked his head into the room and signaled for them to exit.

They were led to the back of the monastery and into a rudimentary kitchen area. Ang and Blake seated themselves at a low table and accepted bowls of steaming stew from the monk.

Glancing out a small window, the monk spun around and used a side door to go outside.

Wearily, Blake exclaimed, "Psychic dreams. What next?"

Ang gulped down big chunks of stew, enjoying every bite.

"Ang, do you have psychic dreams too?"

Ang wrinkled his brow. "What is 'psychic'?"

"That's where you can see the past without having been there or you can see the future. I mean, most people don't even think it's possible."

"I do not have the same ability as the Abbot of Thame. He is a master, while I left gompa very early. Many advanced teachers see past, present, and future—but not me. Perhaps one day."

Blake split a potato with his spoon and lifted the smaller bit to his mouth. "Why did you leave the monastery?"

"My father was a great man, a Tiger of the Snow. He received the medal from the Himalayan Club." Ang reached under his shirt and withdrew a golden medallion suspended on a braided yak hair cord. Blake saw the head of a tiger dwarfing two great mountain peaks. With understated pride, Ang slipped the medal back next to his heart and continued. "He died in a storm during a climb. My mother and my younger sister began carrying then, but still, they suffered. I left the gompa to work and relieve some of the burden my father's death brought."

"So you were about my age when your father died, right?

"Yes."

Blake pressed on in a quiet voice. "And if your father hadn't died, would you still be a monk today?"

"Probably, yes."

His whole world changed as a teenager, just like mine did. My dad didn't die, but he's out of my life—except for our vacation time together. I might even have had a decent time with him if the avalanche hadn't happened and he hadn't decided to send me away. Maybe I should have put up a better fight, proved to him I could take it. Maybe not, Brian seemed messed up. Maybe Dad was right.

Blake and Ang occupied a monk's cell with two bunks, a small window, and a table for a lamp. The window overlooked the waterfall, and Blake liked to watch the stream of falling water. Sometimes he would sit with his back against a cold wall, hypnotized by the sound of the rushing water. His mind cleared, and all the uncertainties of life melted like the liquefied spring snow that ran past his window. Those moments were fleeting, and soon the world would call him back.

The days became routine. Blake shadowed the activities of the monks. He sat in on sessions of chanting and praying, watched rituals with offerings, and listened to monks practicing drums. He understood none of it, but its repetitive nature reassured him. When he could, he would chant or sway with them. Sometimes, they would let him try the drums or cymbals.

By late morning, the younger monks made their way to the river to draw water. Blake loved these outings since it brought him close to nature and the soothing flow of the water. A frigid blast of wind always shook him from the trance induced by chanting away the early mornings. The monks would become gregarious, and although he couldn't understand their speech, he could discern their body language. Playful pushing and teasing and competition over who could carry the most water were all easy concepts he could relate to without language. Occasionally, they would see a small group of white-lipped deer near the water's edge. They showed no fear of humans and would continue to drink even as the boys filled their containers. The monks called them 'sha' and had motioned that they never killed any of the creatures of the forest.

Caught up in the cyclic life of the monastery, Blake lost track of the days. He felt certain he had been there over a week when he went in search of Ang one afternoon.

Most days, Ang disappeared, apparently wanting to be by himself. He always resurfaced at meal times, and late in the afternoons, he helped with repair projects around the compound. By late afternoon, Blake still had seen no sign of him. Making one more circuit through the monastery, he noticed that a small chamber that was usually open had its door tightly shut.

Pressing his ear to the door, Blake tried in vain to hear what might be going on inside. *Is Ang in there? The abbot said I had full access to everything here for my "education." Should I knock? Peek in?*

Blake leaned his shoulder against the heavy door and pushed it ajar a couple of inches. In the dark space, a man lay on the floor. One of the senior monks sat cross-legged near him. *And Ang! What's he doing?* Sitting opposite the monk, Ang held a small metal bowl in his left hand and a wooden baton in his right.

The door scraped across the floor as Blake entered. Ang looked at him, startled, and then motioned for him to join them. Putting the bowl and baton down, Ang rose and pulled Blake away from the prone man and into a darkened corner where the light from the butter lamps did not penetrate.

Blake asked in a whisper, "What's going on?"

"This is a villager who has come for healing. He has a problem with the heart chakra, and now the bowls will be used to make the necessary adjustments."

Blake shook his head, incredulous, and leaned in close. "This guy's got a heart problem and a bowl is going to cure it?"

Ang nodded and added, "You can watch, but you must be silent. The treatment demands no interruption."

Squatting next to Ang, Blake watched with intense curiosity. Of course, it was ridiculous to think that heart conditions could be treated successfully this way. Back home, his dad would be the first to insist on real medical treatment. That would entail drugs and maybe surgical procedures, not a visit to a priest. But he reminded himself he wasn't at home and modern medical treatments were not to be found in these remote mountain areas of Nepal. Subconsciously, he shrugged. What could it hurt? Maybe the placebo effect might even help the poor guy.

The man, probably in his fifties, lay on his back with several blankets cushioning him from the hard, cold floor. His shirt was neatly pulled open, revealing his torso. With his eyes closed, he drew long, slow breaths that inflated his chest. He appeared to be sleeping. Alongside the patient, the monk sat cross-legged, eyes wide open, staring into the distance. *How long will the monk be able to hold that gaze without blinking?* Blake looked into the steady brown eyes so obviously entranced. The monk should have seen him, should have blinked, but he didn't. He stared through Blake, through the wall, beyond the room. Blake's eyes watered, and he blinked several times to clear them.

Surrounding the monk in a half circle, a dozen or so metal bowls of different sizes sat awaiting the healing. The monk moved his hands slowly above the patient, without breaking the trance and without touching the man's body. At the navel, his long bony hands reversed direction and floated back toward the heart. They hung there suspended for a long moment. Apparently satisfied, the monk pulled his arms back and selected a medium-sized tarnished bowl. He cradled it in his palm and picked up a wooden baton.

Ever so lightly, the monk struck the bowl's rim with the stick and drew the baton around its circumference. Blake heard the initial tap but nothing else for a long time. The monk continued to circle the rim with the baton until he coaxed a vibration from within it. The high-pitched sound, faint at first, grew as the monk forced more energy into the alloy. The sound reverberated, rising up the walls where it hung wobbling in the air. Blake wondered if he had felt or heard the sounds first. His ears echoed with the tone even when the monk finished playing. The singing bowl was unlike any other musical instrument he had ever heard. All the percussion instruments Blake could think of worked on a totally different premise. If you hit a drum, a cymbal, or a gong, the sound peaked loudest after the initial hit and then dissipated quickly. The singing bowl reached its auditory climax only after more and more energy was applied. Blake found the whole idea intriguing.

Again and again, the monk struck the bowl and swirled his wrist as if he were mixing cake batter. The patient did not respond to any of the sounds, and after several minutes playing the medium-sized bowl, the monk switched to playing two smaller ones. Those sounds were slightly higher in pitch. Satisfied, the monk again played the medium-sized bowl before moving on to two larger bowls. The larger bowls had diameters over a foot, and instead of holding them, the monk placed them each on a cushion. With a leather-tipped wooden mallet, the monk struck the bowls, one at a time. Each of these produced a deep, pleasing tone.

The monk chose to use only five of the many bowls in this healing. Once finished with them, he sank into a mantra song of low syllables, repeated over and over. Ang began to sway, joining in. The monk picked up a set of brass cymbals and punctuated the end of the mantra before starting the chain of sounds again. The sound of the cymbals revived the patient, who also began to recite the mantra. Two strikes of the cymbals concluded the ceremony, and the prone man opened his eyes.

Sitting up, the patient thanked the monk and rose to leave. The monk threw a branch of juniper onto a small fire and began to gather up the bowls.

Blake turned to Ang. "So now he's healed?"

"Yes, everything that can be done has been accomplished."

Chapter Nineteen

Sitting under an evergreen tree near the waterfall, Blake tried to gather his thoughts on the healing he had just witnessed. Ang sat close and waited. Finally, Ang broke a small twig and began whittling an abstract design.

"You know, Ang, my dad's a doctor so I know a little about medicine. How can a vibration, a sound, cure anything? Does it work because the Sherpa people believe the monk has the power to heal? So it's a mind over matter thing?"

Ang looked up from his whittling. "Your father cures people with special substances you call medicines. We also have herbs and substances that help people get well, but we also have another way to cure the body. I am not a healer and did not study this while I was at the gompa, so my understanding is basic, like that of the average Sherpa. The body is an energy system and the energy flows in a certain way to be healthy. Disturbances in the energy or its flow make people ill. This is a very simple explanation, I know. A healing monk examines the energy flow at the chakras, the way your father uses a thermometer to detect fever."

"I've heard of chakras and Chinese medicine, like acupuncture. But if chakras exist, wouldn't my father and other scientists be using them? Where are the chakras, anyway?"

Ang finished carving a neat braid of knot work around the twig and slipped it into his pocket. "That I can answer. Come with me."

Returning to the small chamber, they found the healing monk crushing leaves in a mortar. Ang spoke a few sentences to the monk, who eyed Blake suspiciously. Then suddenly the monk laughed and nodded as he placed the mortar and pestle aside. He picked up a strand of brown beads and headed for the blankets that had supported the patient with the heart problem. The monk slipped his robe from his shoulders and lay on his back. Ang hurried out of the room while the monk began to chant and move his fingers over the beads that wrapped around his wrist. A few moments later, Ang returned and handed Blake a fistful of dried brown beans.

"What are these for?" Blake asked.

"You are going to mark the chakras with those."

Taking Blake by the elbow, Ang led him to the monk's side, where they squatted down.

"The chakra points are areas of intense energy discharge. You will feel the energy with your hands."

Blake looked at the beans in his hands. "There are this many chakras?"

"I have given you more beans than you will need, but you will determine the number of chakras and their locations in my scientific experiment." Ang beamed with pride as he revealed his idea.

"Well, I'll give it a try, but, believe me, I've touched people before and I've never felt any energy coming out of me or anyone else."

"What you will sense is heat. You are looking for hot spots." Ang crossed his arms over his chest, confident in his experiment.

"Hot spots. Okay, then, here goes. Oops, do I need to say any mumbo-jumbo, maybe abracadabra before I start?" Blake laughed and set the beans down. He raised his hands as he'd seen the monk do.

Ang ignored the insolence, confident of success.

Blake moved his hands over the healing monk's body without touching him. He felt nothing.

Exasperated, Ang sighed and pushed Blake's hands to within four inches of touching the man's chest. "Now, go slowly. When you find a spot, place a bean there."

Blake smirked but said nothing. He moved his hands to the man's head and moved downward as slowly as he could. "Should I close my eyes?"

"It is not necessary. But, you may if you wish," Ang answered.

Scanning the monk's face, Blake still could detect nothing, but when he approached the center of the throat, he felt a slight warming. Surprised, he backed up to the forehead and moved down again. As he paused, the area grew warmer. He moved down a few inches and the air cooled. His hands shot back to the throat, searching for warmth.

Blake's voice quivered. "I think I found one.... Is this right?"

Ang chuckled. The monk raised an eyelid.

"I am not going to tell you if you are correct or not. Just place the beans," Ang said.

Blake put a bean on the monk's throat and continued scanning. He moved down and placed more beans at the center of the man's chest at the same level as the physical heart, on the navel, and on the genital area. Excited by being able to sense the heat zones, Blake returned to the monk's head to do one last pass to insure that he had everything correctly placed. Warmth rose from the crown of the head and extended over the forehead. Blake put a bean there and moved on. He completed the experiment and looked at Ang hopefully.

"I can't believe it, but you're right! I can feel hot spots. Did I get them all?"

"We shall soon see," Ang answered. He went to a table and opened a book by lifting its wooden cover. He lifted several parchment pages and set them aside before he retrieved what he wanted. Returning to Blake, he held up a yellowed page with a block print drawing of a man. On the man, lotus flowers marked the chakra sites.

Blake took the sheet and compared each site to his own positioning of the beans.

"I got them all! Okay, there are five chakra sites and I found them. Why don't doctors back home know about this? I mean, you can FEEL them. They're real!"

Ang shook his head, unable to answer Blake's question.

The next afternoon while Blake sat near the waterfall, a young monk came to fetch him. He was led back to the abbot's chamber where the white macaw screamed and fussed while the lama sat reading ancient texts.

Blake entered the room, and the abbot rose and smoothed the agitated bird's feathers, calming him into submission.

"Ah, good!" the lama exclaimed. "I have been wanting to practice my English. Please sit."

Blake clumsily assumed the cross-legged, lotus position on the floor as the abbot took his seat on a dais, bird on shoulder. "Please tell me about your home," the lama requested.

"My home? I live in Ohio now, but before that I lived in California. In the United States. I live with my mom, and I'm in the tenth grade."

The macaw grabbed a clawful of the abbot's robe and raised it up and let it go. Amused, it did it again. "Yes, I know of California. Sunshine and the ocean! Sea World."

"You know about Sea World?"

"I have traveled to Delhi and conversed with American monks from your California. Perhaps one day I will visit."

"Thame is a long way from California." Blake shifted uncomfortably. "I miss home sometimes, but I know I'll be leaving when the climbing season is over. Were you born here in Thame?"

The lama's smile faded and he shook his head. "My home is Amdo, in Tibet. It is close to fifty years ago that I came to Thame after escaping the Chinese. I was to return with a delegation some years ago, but that never happened. So many left Tibet. Like chaff from wheat, we were cast to the winds." The abbot raised his finger and the bird took it into his mouth.

Trying to lighten the mood, Blake pointed to the macaw and asked, "What's his name?"

"His name is Chung. He was a gift and now is a good friend." The old man rubbed the macaw's comb affectionately.

The melancholy sound of a conch being blown signaled the start of prayers for the gompa. The abbot escorted Blake to the door.

"Thank you for helping me practice my English. Ang has told me you will leave tomorrow. I wish you a safe and happy journey."

Out in the hallway, Blake stood to the side, allowing a group of young monks to pass. Ang had not mentioned that they were leaving. Where would they go now? Why could they never stay in one location for any length of time? When he had finally settled into the routine of life here, Ang decided once again to uproot him. Blake shook his head. It just wasn't fair that Ang called all the shots.

Blake found Ang in the deserted kitchen. A large pot boiled furiously, reminding him of his rising anger. Ang sat on the floor working on an overturned table. He hammered at one of the table legs and then turned the table right side up.

With an air of annoyance, Blake launched into his tirade. "Hey, the abbot just said you told him we're leaving tomorrow."

"That is correct," Ang said shaking the table to check its strength.

Blake crossed his arms in defiance and continued. "Well, you never mentioned it to me! Why is it so important to keep moving? I'm used to things around here, so why don't we stay for a while?"

"For what purpose?"

"What do you mean 'for what purpose'? The purpose is to kill some time before we have to meet my dad. Why brave the wilderness when we can stay here and be comfortable? Eventually, we'll have to go, I know. But until then, this is a safe place, and the food's okay. We can hang out here a month or so and then leave for Katmandu. How 'bout it?"

Ang turned to face Blake. "No, we must leave. The gompa has extended us many hospitalities, but there is more to our journey. Your obligation and my obligation to the Rinpoche cannot be fulfilled here, and so we must leave."

Blake shook his head violently. "This idea that I'm going to change my mind about the camera...it's just not going to happen. You can keep shuttling me around the whole country, making me tired and oh, so confused, but I'm telling you—I'm not buying into it! I'm not changing my mind. I'm going to collect my camera and my pictures and I'm out of here for good." He stormed from the room.

He ran down the passageway. He could hear the muffled sounds of chants, drums, and cymbals becoming fainter as he moved away. Through the main entrance, he burst out into the world. The peacock strutting on the walkway gave way and cleared the path for him. Looking for a place to be alone, Blake circled the monastery and headed for the waterfall. He sank to his knees near the water's edge and felt the cool river spray splatter his face. The thunderous crash of thousands of gallons of water did not soothe his spirits. He felt full of the same rage the water released as it hit the bottom of the falls.

How could his life be so out of control? How could a divorce and some drugs have brought him to this place? Why did Dad do it to him? If only things had stayed the way they were. He would still be in California. Blake ripped up some grass and twisted it his fist before throwing the wad toward the water. He tried to calm down and consider his position, but his anger only grew. Ang called the shots because his father wanted it that way. Dad had sent him away and he had to obey. What other choice was there? Blake pushed the hair back from his face and sighed. But that was not the only reason Ang had control. Ang was in charge because he, Blake, had made a deal with the Rinpoche. A deal he should never have had to make. His anger slowly shifted to himself. *I made the choice. I'm here because I agreed. Maybe I shouldn't have. But I did. It's my fault. Ang's in charge because I put him there.*

Blake sat curled in a ball holding his knees as he considered his part in the whole mess. He wanted to be home so desperately that he closed his eyes and forced himself to see it. The image of the condo with the carport flanked by the resin goose, dressed for each holiday, made him smirk. He remembered his mom's car filled with the "open house" signs each Saturday, and he remembered Mom. Mom who had changed so much since their move. At first, she had been so happy to go back to her small hometown in Ohio, and then one day it had all changed. He had never known what had happened, but she turned quiet and sad. A couple of weeks after that, Grandpa died. Massive stroke. Grandma had found him on the floor in the barn.

Long after the sun had set, Blake climbed the hill back up to the monastery. He found that the evening meal had been served and cleared. Ang pored over trekking maps back in their room. Blake slid into bed and pulled the blankets up over his head.

Snow covered the Thame Valley that night. Standing in front of the gompa, Blake looked down on the sleepy village frosted white. The air, heavy with moisture, sent a shiver down his back. He tugged at his jacket zipper, sealing himself off from the chill, and then pulled his hat down around his ears. With the monks busy with early morning chores, Ang and Blake set off on their solitary journey.

Ahead, the rocky trail wound north. Blake slipped numerous times as his boots hit rock and failed to gain traction. He watched as Ang, nimble as a mountain goat, navigated the rough terrain without ever losing his footing. Finally, Blake broke a branch from a nearby shrub and fashioned a walking stick. He just managed to keep up with Ang using the extra support. Physical exertion warmed him as they moved higher into the mountain pass. Overhead, an eagle owl screamed, and Ang pointed. "Wookpa!"

The only form of wildlife they had seen so far punctuated the fact that they were truly alone in nature. Blake was again reminded of how dependent he was on Ang.

Skirting a narrow ridge, Blake clung to the overhang that protected the walkway. Ang moved forward only inches from the edge, seemingly oblivious to this precarious part of the path. Even more unsettling were his pauses where he stopped and looked out over the side of the cliff. Blake did everything he could to focus on the trail and never, ever look down. Thankfully, the trail grew wider and descended at a comfortable pace. He relaxed and eased himself into the center of the path. As he did so, he noticed small footprints that crossed in front of him and disappeared over the side of a ridge.

"Ang, wait a sec! What's this?" Blake pointed to the animal prints.

Ang joined Blake and studied the prints. "Those are Chiru."

"Chiru? What's that, a goat?"

"No. Chiru!" Ang pointed to the next rock outcropping. "There!"

A half dozen beige and white antelope with black horns grazed in the distance. Their black faces turned to face Blake and Ang. Skittish, one of the larger ones started to climb higher, and as it did, a small avalanche of rocks tumbled into a canyon below. That panicked the rest of the herd, who then struggled to move higher.

"How do they survive up here? What do they eat? Wookpa?" Blake chuckled at his joke.

Ang shook his head and returned to the trail. Leaving the Chiru behind, they circled east and found a green valley spread before them with a cold, blue lake carved into the emerald grasslands. Sturdy shrubs and tasseled grasses swayed in the gentle breeze. Bright sunshine illuminated the crisp indigo sky as they approached the water. Black headed gulls cried flying low over the lake. Blake stepped over tiny pink primroses with yellow centers. Pale blue poppies bloomed from tiny stalks with bristly leaves. The intense colors reminded Blake of a kaleidoscope he'd once owned. Setting his pack down, he retrieved his camera and snapped shots of the flowers, the birds, and the lake. Ang gathered a few branches from a prickly looking bush.

Setting his brush pile down, Ang unwrapped a strong-smelling cheese and handed Blake a piece. They shared some dried yak meat while sitting at the edge of the lake. Blake hauled out his water bottle and drank, watching various water birds gather and frolic. Across the lake, a group of white-lipped deer drank nervously. Ang ignited the brush pile with a lighter, saying, "This is an offering to the yoklu spirits who live in the lake." They both watched as the branches sparked and the desiccated pile burst into flame and quickly died out. Together they sat on the ground and looked out over the lake.

Uncomfortable in the silence, Blake asked, "So, weren't you going to explain how Buddhists stop wanting things? And how someone can overcome those misperceptions of reality? I think I could use a little help with that about now. Just saying."

Ang nodded. "Yes. It is through practicing a set of principles that we free ourselves from these desires and begin to understand the underlying nature of reality. The Noble Eightfold Path guides our daily life."

"Sounds a lot like the Ten Commandments that Christians follow."

"Perhaps it is similar." Assuming the role of teacher, Ang continued. "First is correct view. Buddhists must understand key religious concepts and work to correct wrong views. The most important wrong view is believing that the physical and mental appearances of the individual translate into a truly existent person."

Blake gulped a mouthful of water. "That goes back to the idea of illusion and what's real. So a person isn't really...real. Getting a grasp on reality in this country is tough."

"Do you doubt what you see?"

Blake chuckled. "And hear, smell, taste.... Stuff I'd never believe at home...sometimes seems reasonable here."

"Ah. Good! That means the first principle is taking root. We move on to the second, that of correct intention. A person must commit to the ultimate goal of enlightenment. To do this on a practical level, a person must renounce worldly things, avoid harming others, and actively pursue enlightenment."

"Okay, got it. What's next?"

"Next is correct speech. To cultivate stability of mind, a person must speak truthfully in a pleasant way. Speech is a manifestation of the mind."

"I thought you were going to say that swearing or taking the lord's name in vain wasn't allowed, but I guess that's Christian."

"It would apply here also, since swearing and cursing the gods would not help to develop pleasant speech. This is one I struggle with when I am carrying and things are not going well," Ang smirked.

Finishing his last bit of jerky, Blake stood up and scooped up a handful of rocks. He skipped a few stones across the smooth surface of the lake.

"Continuing, the fourth principle is correct action. Of course, monks have many rules instilling monastic discipline. For the rest of us, correct action focuses on not doing things based on negative mental attitudes. So no killing, no stealing, no lying, no sexual improprieties, no drugs."

"All that rolled into one. The Ten Commandments cover most of that. If this is only the fourth rule, Buddhists must have a lot of restrictions."

"Perhaps. The next concerns correct livelihood. A person must make a living at work that does not violate any of the rules. Work cannot involve killing, neither person nor animal. Jobs that exploit or cheat others are not correct livelihood. Correct livelihood allows a positive mental condition."

Blake plopped down next to Ang. "It makes sense that immoral jobs aren't allowed under this system."

"Now, we shall deal with the last three rules. Everything that went before concerned developing proper attitude and action. The last three deal with the importance of meditation. Correct effort is the sixth rule. Steady and consistent effort is required to make progress through meditation. So one must make effort at this."

Blake nodded but didn't interrupt.

"Once correct effort is made, a person must cultivate correct mindfulness. One moves from a state of confusion and random thoughts to develop clarity. Ultimately, the goal is to control the mental processes and attitudes."

"How do you do this?" Blake asked.

"There are teachers and texts outlining techniques for all this."

"It sounds pretty complicated."

"Yes, but many lifetimes are provided to perfect it. The last principle is called correct concentration. A calm and concentrated mind can focus on a single object without distraction. Advanced meditative states are then possible."

Blake dug his heel into the loose soil and moved it back and forth, thinking. "Some things seem really easy to understand and other parts seem complicated, especially the ones dealing with meditation. I think it would take lifetimes to learn everything."

Ang smiled, getting to his feet. "I am through being the teacher today. We should get moving. I know a shelter, not too far away, we can use for the night."

Chapter Twenty

The afternoon sun beat down on Blake's shoulders. At lower altitude with no wind, the milder climate made him think of spring. The colorful bloom of the alpine meadow, although exotic in form, drew his mind back to being with his grandfather.

After his grandfather retired, he had taken up flower gardening. He'd pore over gardening catalogs looking for just the right rose bush to put here or the right shade plant to try there. The week he died he'd shown Blake a picture of a new purple English rose he thought he might buy for the arbor he had planned. Blake remembered how his grandmother would shake her head, still trying to get used to the man who for years had thought growing flowers was a waste of time and a "waste of good growing soil." Every once in a while he'd even mention he was considering joining the gardening society. His grandmother would give him that look each time, knowing the gardening society consisted of a bunch of mostly elderly, mostly widowed women. Then Grandpa would wink at him. Blake missed him since his sudden death.

Walking next to Ang, he said, "The flowers remind me of my grandpa."

"He likes flowers?"

"He used to. He died a couple of months ago..."

Ang nodded and after a moment said, "Once Lord Buddha came upon a woman who was suffering with the death of a child. He sent her to collect mustard seeds from every home that had not had a loss of a loved one. She returned empty handed. He showed her that she was not alone in her grief and that death is a part of life."

"I know that, but it's hard anyway."

"Yes, difficult. For me, no death was ever as hard as that of my father. When it is sudden and unexpected, it is even more painful."

With hope, Blake asked, "But you got over it?"

"You deal with life, you go on. Over time, the loss becomes less noticeable. It hurts less and you hope for a pleasant rebirth for the loved one."

Blake nodded. "My grandmother thinks he's in heaven. I don't know. I'm not so sure. Heaven sounds just as strange as the idea of reincarnation. So either I believe that my grandfather is sitting on a cloud playing a harp or I believe he's coming back to earth as a child." He sighed and a moment passed in silence. "It's weird to think of him being reborn as a baby. But maybe. Maybe someday I'll be on my way somewhere and see a little kid who reminds me of him and I'd recognize him." Blake's eyes sparkled with moisture, tears he held back.

The pair had almost walked their way out of the valley. Ahead lay more rough landscape to be covered before nightfall. Rodent-like creatures, the size of beavers, scurried between boulders carrying clumps of vegetation.

"Your father mentioned that you and your mother had moved back to her hometown after the divorce," Ang said.

"Yeah, not that there were a whole lot of options. Mom used to be a real estate agent, and she thought she could go back to it and be near my grandparents again."

Ang glanced sideways at Blake. "You were not happy with that choice?"

Blake shrugged. "Didn't matter. Nobody even asked me. Dad went off to do his thing, as usual, and Mom...had limited options. Once the divorce went through, she spent a week with my grandparents and came back with the idea of moving there. She seemed really happy about it. I never was. It was culture shock moving from California to the Midwest and me not knowing anybody else, new to the school, well, it was tough."

"But soon, you made friends?"

"No, not really. I suffered through the first quarter pretty much on my own. Mom took her job really seriously, so I'd be alone or sometimes at my grandparents'. But second quarter, I met Slade and we started hanging out together. Slade's cool, knows his way around. We like the same things: music, counter-culture, Goth stuff."

"Your dad said there were problems and he thought you should spend time with him."

"Yeah, problems! Problems he caused. If it wasn't for the divorce, I wouldn't have had my life ripped open. I'd still be in California with my old friends hanging out on the beach."

"You sound angry."

"I have a right to be angry."

Ang met Blake's eyes. "So angry, you started taking harmful substances?"

"God, he told you that! He can't even shut his mouth about my business. I smoked a couple of joints with Slade. Big deal! Nobody would even know, except that Mom found an extra joint in my jeans. And she freaked. That was when she was in her "depression." Any other time she would have been rational and sat me down for a long talk. Instead, she calls my dad, who's getting ready for his trip of a lifetime. That's how I wound up on Mount Everest!"

Ang smirked. "Small correction. You have never been on Mount Everest; you were at Base Camp and only for a few days. Big difference."

"Yeah, Base Camp. Anyway, I shouldn't have had to come. Marijuana is no big deal when you consider that meth is the drug of choice in the heartland. Mom should have seen that, but I don't know. Her behavior became so unpredictable. She went from this totally together, totally driven person one day, to a depressed, can't handle anything mess..."

The trail became steep and the footing difficult. Ang pointed to two large rocks at the edge of the trail. Blake sat and peeled off his pack. He gulped down some water as Ang squatted nearby.

Cautiously, Ang asked, "You never knew why your mother became so overwhelmed?"

Blake shook his head and wiped away some water that had dribbled down his chin.

Ang frowned and looked away, back into the valley they had just left. Blake could see him struggling, but he waited patiently.

"Truth is a relative thing, based on our own perspective. I know you are angry with your father over the divorce. Perhaps that is justified. I wish your father were here now. Or, better still, your mother." Ang brought his hands together, fingers lightly touching, forming a pyramid. "Your father has told me certain things and normally, I would keep them to myself. But seeing your uncertainty and pain, I am forced to consider other options."

Sighing, he continued. "Before the divorce, your mother resumed a relationship with a man she had met during her college years. She returned to her hometown for all the reasons you outlined and one you were unaware of. That man lives in your town. Your mom thought that if she moved back, that there would be a future with him. I suspect that was why she was initially very happy. Unable to leave his wife and small children, this man broke off seeing your mother."

Blake shoulders slumped and he moaned. "That's why she got so depressed! I thought maybe some of it was my grandfather's death, but that didn't make a lot of sense because she changed before he died."

Recapping his water bottle, Blake considered the information he had just been given. It all made sense now. He could fill in the holes and grasp at least some of it. He felt relieved knowing the truth, but in some ways it carried with it even more unresolved emotions. If Ang's story was true, that meant his father wasn't solely responsible for the divorce. When, exactly, had his mother begun this affair with this old boyfriend? Where was he during all this, and why did it take a Sherpa, in the middle of the Himalayas, to tell him about it? Why hadn't Mom told him, or why hadn't Dad at least told him? Was Dad protecting her? Was Dad protecting him? Was Dad the hero in all this? Should he be blaming Mom for what had gone wrong?

Blake thrust his water bottle into his pack and wrestled it onto his back. He and Ang set off up the rocky path. The rich colors of the meadow were replaced by light brown hues. The dusty foothills collected the broken remains of boulders at their base, making their travel difficult. Sunlight bounced off the rocks, while other areas remained in shadow.

The barrenness of the countryside, and the news Blake tried to process, darkened his mood. *I should have known this. I should have seen the signs. Why didn't I just ask? Am I the only one on the planet who didn't know my mother had an affair? At least I was right about Grandpa's death; that wasn't what caused the depression. That idiot dumped her, and that changed her. I'm sure Grandpa's death didn't help. And Dad. Maybe none of this was really his fault. Maybe I've been blaming the wrong parent.*

The hillsides drew closer to the trail, blocking much of the sun. They were in a narrow pass with steep cliff faces on both sides. Without the sun to warm the pass, Blake felt chilled to the bone in the desolate valley. The cold and darkness, contrasting with the sun they had left behind, made Blake think about Ang's spirits. If spirits inhabited the waters, they also had to exist here, in this creepy place.

"Ang!" Blake called. "Are there spirits in here?"

Ang stopped and waited for Blake to come alongside him. "Of course, spirits are all around us, all the time." Ang waved his arm, gesturing at the rocks that surrounded them.

"Here are the nyen. You can feel them. I am saying prayers to make our passage safe."

"So these nyen are bad?"

"They can be. They can bring sickness and death. Do not worry. The prayers are powerful and we travel with the protection of the Rinpoche. Still, we must keep moving."

The cold and talk of the nyen encouraged Blake to walk faster. Soon they had passed out of the tight valley and moved into a more hospitable environment. The same dry, dark hills lined the trail, but with the sun and some puffy white clouds, Blake felt the nyen had lost their powers. If they ever had powers to begin with.

Blake readjusted his pack. "How much farther?"

"Not long now."

The trail began to climb ever so slightly. After another hour or so, they had walked into a crescent-shaped valley. At this higher elevation, snow-capped peaks could be seen in the distance. A fast-running stream sliced through the basin, and opposite the water, a sheer, sandstone cliff showed excavated holes.

Blake pointed and shouted, "Caves!"

"Our home tonight," Ang answered.

They had reached their destination. Blake had never spent a night in a cave, and he was anxious to find shelter and get his pack off. The cave Ang chose was not the one closest to the ground They climbed above two of the lower openings to a cave about ten feet off the ground. Standing in the doorway, Blake peered into the darkness. Ang brought forth a flashlight and pointed it inside. Not much bigger than Blake's room back home, the cave had a flat floor and a nice seven-foot ceiling. It would make a comfortable space for the night. He felt indebted to the person who had carved the cave, perhaps hundreds of years earlier. Blake slid his pack off and crumpled to the floor. Ang walked around the perimeter, looking at the painted religious images that covered the cave's surfaces. Stashed along the back wall, brush similar to what Ang had burned as an offering was piled floor to ceiling.

"This is a monk's cave?" Blake called out.

Ang nodded, still moving the light over the artwork. Finally, he approached Blake and removed his pack. "The cave was probably carved by a yogin. Some of the paintings are recent, though. I was here about five years ago, and I can recognize the new work."

"Monks still come to these faraway places? Why?"

"Some want to take retreat to get away from monastic life, and sometimes the retreat is required for higher spiritual progress."

Blake shifted his pack to use it as a pillow and lay down. "How long would someone live out here on their own?"

"Years." Ang dug in his pack and brought out some canned food. "Soup or stew?"

Sleepily, Blake answered, "Soup, later."

The scent of chicken soup roused Blake from his sleep. Ang had built a fire using the brush from the back of the cave. He stirred the soup and poured it into cups. Stiff from lying on the hard rock floor, Blake stretched and eased himself into a sitting position. He reached out for the cup Ang offered. His rigid fingers wrapped around the hot mug, soothing his joints.

Outside, the sun had begun its descent. A stillness hung over the valley as the land was bathed in gold and crimson beams. Blake finished the soup and downed some water.

"It's amazing how good canned soup tastes here. Back home I hardly ever eat soup."

Ang sipped his tea. "My wife makes wonderful meals when I am at home, but out here we must make do."

Blake went to the cave's entrance and sat down on its edge. Beyond the water lay a vast barren plateau. He found himself alone in twilight.

Suddenly, in the distance Blake saw movement. A dark spot raced across the flat landscape. It covered a huge distance in mere seconds. Blake wondered if it was an animal or perhaps an optical illusion. He looked away, he looked back. It was still there so it wasn't an optical illusion. It veered off, moving at a forty-five-degree angle away from him. A few more seconds and it reversed itself, coming toward him again. Unnerved, Blake jumped to his feet and ran to Ang.

"There's something out there, moving fast! Really fast! Get your binoculars!"

Ang sprang to his feet and quickly recovered his binoculars.

They ran to the cave's opening. Blake grabbed the glasses from Ang and raised them to look.

"Where?" shouted Ang.

"On the plateau, over there!" Blake yelled back.

Blake focused the binoculars on the ridge where he'd last seen movement. Quickly, he scanned in the direction in which the thing had been moving.

"There!" Ang shouted.

Blake looked out from the glasses to see what Ang indicated. There! The same black object, hurling forward. Blake got the position and thrust the binoculars toward it. He spun his body to keep up with the motion and focused the glasses by turning the center wheel. The image resolved into a dark man with a brown loin cloth, weighted down with chains, traveling at fantastic speed. Because he moved so quickly, his legs were never clearly visible. His feet did not appear to touch the ground and instead of running, the movement more closely resembled a bouncing ball.

"It's a man!" Blake screamed.

Ang wrestled the binoculars from Blake and took a look.

"How can he do that? It's not human. People don't run like that! Even an Olympic runner wouldn't move *that* fast. For God's sake, he's hopping!" Blake said.

Blake watched the black spot of a man reverse himself and return in the direction he had come.

Ang said nothing but watched the progress of the bouncing ball through the binoculars. Impatient, Blake grabbed the glasses back and stared as the man sped off out of sight.

Blake let the glasses fall to his chest where the cord prevented them from falling to the ground. He scanned the plateau for more movement. Ang sat at the cave's entrance, legs dangling free, shaking his head.

Blake threw himself down next to Ang. "What the hell was that?"

Ang drew a long, deep breath. "I have seen many things, especially in the mountains, but I have never seen that before. At gompa, there was talk. Talk of training for a few special men..."

"And..." Blake said, trying to draw out more from the hesitant Sherpa.

"They are called lung-gom-pa runners. Their purpose is to gather up demons that threaten us. I believe we just saw a monk in training."

Blake nodded. "In training. How do you train for this superhuman feat?"

"It is a secret tantric practice that I am not familiar with. I know it involves energy manipulation using yoga breathing and mantras. Over time, the body is lightened and the practitioner learns to jump very high."

Quietly, Blake said, "But Ang, the guy's feet never touched the ground."

Ang exhaled loudly. "I know. From Tibetan legend, it is said that the body becomes so light that it is possible to sit on an ear of barley and not bend the stalk."

"Did you see the chains?"

"Yes. Jumping yoga allows levitation. The chains, the chains hold him down."

Chapter Twenty-One

"The chains hold him down." Blake propped his elbow on his knee and rested his chin in his hand. The longer he traveled into this land, the more bizarre things became. How was he supposed to believe that a holy man needs chains to keep from floating away? Yeti, aliens, prophetic dreams, magic healing bowls, levitating yogis—where did it end?

Sometimes, it felt like he had been swept up into a fantasy realm, stranger than a trip into outer space. He snickered. Outer space was easy to comprehend in comparison. Good, old fashioned science guided and explained space travel. Nothing seemed to explain anything he experienced. Time and time again, his beliefs were turned upside down without explanation. Like an astronaut who had had no preparation and no NASA support team to help him, he felt overwhelmed and tired by the new challenges that presented themselves on a regular basis. Blake sat frozen by his thoughts on the ledge of the cave.

The last rays of the setting sun shone over the valley, quickly receding. The night would be clear and cold. Blake heard Ang rise and throw more brush on the dying fire. Finally, as his extremities grew numb and his backside ached from sitting still so long, he retreated to the fire. He spread out his sleeping bag and fell into a fitful sleep.

Throughout the night he awoke with nightmares. In the first, he was being pursued by yogis with chains who jumped across the landscape like bouncing basketballs. He had been terrified trying to outrun them, and sweat poured down his face. Blake mopped the perspiration with his mitten and tried to settle his racing heart. He focused on his breathing and pushed the disturbing images from his mind. As he drifted off, he saw an operating room with a medical team surrounding him. Blake looked down and saw his chest cut open, revealing his pulsing heart. In desperation, he searched the room for his dad. The medical personnel morphed into monks dressed in burgundy robes, chanting and playing singing bowls. A primal scream shattered the image, and Blake flung himself up onto an elbow. Cold and scared, he scooted closer to the fire. He tore his mittens off and stretched his fingers over the fire's embers. He vowed not to sleep again that night.

Blake stared at the fire, watching the light flicker and move rhythmically. The heat warmed him, the crackling sounds calmed him, and the colors drew him in. When he first awoke, the fire had been burning red with tinges of yellow and occasional orange. He pulled his hands back, and the fire leapt up and burst blue. The electric blue hovered for a moment before changing into various hues of green. The green melted into yellow and then the fire went crazy, displaying rainbow-striped peaks. Optical illusions? Fires didn't behave this way. Not normally. Pulled into the light show, Blake didn't have the energy to fight its effects. Although only moments before, he had declared he wouldn't sleep, he felt himself lie back down. He felt calm and oddly detached from his body. He tingled all over, but he wasn't afraid. He closed his eyes and surrendered to sleep. A single image appeared before him. The face of the Rinpoche, brown eyes fixed, chanting. Blake slept.

Early the next morning, Ang shook him awake.

Blake turned over mumbling, "Another five minutes." *I'd like another week of sleep, tucked into my own bed at home.* He drifted off, but soon Ang appeared, back in his face. *No use, I'll have to get up.*

Beyond the extinguished fire, Blake saw the gray valley still sleeping. A few tentative rays of yellow penetrated the dusk in the distance. With a yawn, he pulled himself up and reached for a hot cup of tea that Ang handed him. An energy bar and raisins made for a very exotic breakfast that morning. Maybe Ang had sensed his exhaustion, both the physical and emotional, and decided to try to improve his mood. The odd thing was that it worked. The tea warmed his soul, and the raisins were like candy; sweet, mushy, and chewy. For the first time in a while, Blake felt contented, even happy.

Exhilarated, he launched into an account of the previous night's events. "Had a dream last night. It was really crazy. First, a bunch of lung-gom-pa monks were chasing me. Then the fire exploded like fireworks. Finally, I dreamed the Rinpoche saved me."

Ang tossed raisins into his mouth and chewed vigorously. "Interesting. Dreams have much importance."

"Well, I think my dreams were strange because of what we saw last night. Believe me, I don't dream like that at home."

Ang nodded, picked up his few remaining belongings, and stuffed them into his pack. Blake did the same and then hoisted the pack onto his back. Outside the cave, the valley started to warm as the sun rose higher.

"Where are we going?" Blake said.

"There is another gompa at the base of a pass. We go there next."

"Another monastery. What a surprise!" Biting his bottom lip, Blake wondered if he should challenge Ang's plan. He quickly dismissed the idea. So far, he'd had no influence on where Ang chose to travel.

They walked northeast, exiting the valley of caves. The trail inclined slightly, and ahead, Blake knew, lay tall mountains. The dusty trail soon became more difficult as he had to negotiate sharp rocks that jutted up at irregular intervals. Ang moved at his own sure-footed pace, gliding over the trail as if he had been born to do nothing else. Blake caught his boot on a rock and careened through the air. He landed with a thud. Ang glanced over his shoulder to find Blake sprawled out on the ground. Luckily, with all the clothing he had on, he was more embarrassed than hurt. He picked himself up, readjusted his pack, and continued. *Why do I always have to look like an idiot? Will it ever be Ang's turn?*

Several hours following the rough trail eventually led them to a ridge where Blake viewed the monastery for the first time. Perched atop a high peak, swathed in clouds, the monastery looked more like an impenetrable fortress than a religious center. A high wall encircled the stacked, rectangular buildings. High enough to kiss the face of God, if Buddhists had believed in that God. Blake wondered why the gompa had been built so inaccessibly. Behind the fortress lay even higher, snow-clad mountains.

"That is Denyatil," Ang said.

Blake sighed, realizing that the hardest part of today's journey still lay ahead. "Why do these places always have to be so hard to reach?"

Ang shrugged and led Blake up the path to the monastery. In several places, they negotiated steep inclines by climbing roughly hewn steps cut vertically into the mountainside. The air grew thinner, and Blake felt his body strain under the challenge. He grabbed Ang's arm, huffing and puffing, and they stopped to rest. The clouds shifted and they became engulfed in fog. Blake felt the moisture on his face and wiped the icy dew from the tip of his nose. He extended his hand out to his side and watched his extremity disappear mystically in the vapor. Face to face, he could still see Ang. Blake took a step back, and Ang evaporated as if he had never been there.

"Stand still!" Ang yelled. "Let the mist recede."

The words had hardly escaped Ang's mouth when suddenly the fog lifted and floated straight up.

"Awesome! Now, that was cool," Blake said.

Irritated, Ang warned, "If that happens again, stand still. I can't go back and tell your father that you fell off a mountain because of a cloud!"

"All right already! I'll stand still. Compared to what we've been through, a cloud is nothing."

"Visibility and weather play a big role in mountain survival. Do not underestimate it. Do not let your guard down. Overconfidence has killed men."

Is this me, or is he overreacting? I took one step he didn't approve of. What's the big deal?

Ang and Blake pushed up and over the last ridge that separated them from the compound. Ahead stood the outer protective wall, shut off from the world by a thick, wooden door. Without hesitation, Ang took the medieval iron knocker in his hand and rapped loudly. The door swung open and a young novice monk stood shyly behind it.

Ang exchanged a few words with the monk, and they were led through the grounds. They passed several single-story buildings and a chorten draped in the familiar yellow, green, red, white, and blue prayer flags.

As they approached the main facility, Ang pulled Blake aside. "Let me visit with the monks alone. You stay here and I will return for you."

Blake watched Ang follow the young monk to the entrance of the monastery and, after slipping off his shoes, he disappeared into its depths. Blake took a seat on the cold stone stairs and looked out over the gompa. From behind him, the deep melancholy sound of a conch being blown sounded from atop the roof. Blake twisted and shielded his eyes from the sun searching for the source of the sound. His attention was drawn back by the sound of shuffling feet in the courtyard. A dozen monks assembled before him, all barefoot, all draped in white repas. Blake shivered just looking at them. An older monk, similarly attired and jangling prayer beads, barked a command and the group marched out of view. Blake snickered. *I hope they're going to go put on more clothes! How can they stand around here barefoot?*

Ang returned a few moments later and informed him that the lama had welcomed them and invited them to stay.

"Why couldn't I go in with you?" Blake asked following Ang to one of the nearby buildings.

"The lama here is old and does not favor surprises. He did not know we were coming, and I hoped to lessen the shock. It went quite well, and he has offered his hospitality. Come. We will eat."

Blake smelled food before they even arrived at the doorway of the gompa kitchen. As he drew nearer, some of the aromas were good, but whiffs of others made him gag. Blake threw himself around the corner of the building, freeing himself from the assault of the rotten odors. He heard Ang exchange a few words with someone at the door. A hand holding a bowl came around the corner. Blake took it and inhaled. Thankfully, it smelled like roasted yak meat.

Ang joined him, and they ate the meal in silence. Blake watched a white puffy patch begin to descend on them again. Some of the two-story buildings lost their top floors in the fog, but at least he and Ang could still see each other.

Ang wiped his forehead and said carefully, "I apologize for my short temper with you when we were in the mist."

Blake nodded and in mid-mouthful said, "Sure, no problem."

"Once, when I was quite young and had just started carrying, I camped overnight on a ridge with others who were carrying. We woke up in a cloud. One fellow, from Katmandu, stepped out from his tent and was never seen again."

Blake listened, wide-eyed.

Ang collected the bowls. "We found his body on the trip down."

While Ang left the bowls near the kitchen, Blake meandered up the path. Calling over his shoulder, he said, "Can we take a look around? I saw a group of monks go around that way." Blake stripped off his pack and left it in a corner where two buildings met.

Ang let Blake lead him behind the main monastery building. They passed more two-story, white structures built in the traditional flat-roofed style. Continuing, they saw the group of monks across the way, sitting on a hilly knoll where a fast mountain stream ran. Still clad only in lightweight repa robes, Blake wondered why the senior monk had chosen to hold training out of doors. Although the sun shone brightly that afternoon, the altitude and time of year didn't seem conducive to outside events, especially while half naked. Blake wanted to get as close to the group as possible, and when Ang placed a hand on his shoulder he knew he had reached that limit.

Blake sat down and Ang squatted. They both listened to the lama's singsong voice, apparently instructing the young monks. The way he moved his hands and eyes told Blake he wasn't chanting. Still, Blake could only guess what he was saying. He wished Ang could translate, but he knew any talking would disturb the monks. He had no choice but to sit still and watch in ignorance. Time passed, and still the lama droned on and on. Blake considered signaling Ang that it was time to leave when suddenly the young monks all rose and removed their repas. Blake shot a quizzical look to Ang, but Ang was unmoved. Blake had no idea what they were doing.

The adepts moved to the icy stream and submerged their robes.

Washing day? No soap? Maybe it's some kind of ritual cleansing.

The monks wrung out the garments and returned to where they had been sitting. As a group, each of them put their repas back on and sat cross-legged at the lama's feet. No one shivered or showed the slightest reaction to the cold. Blake watched a young monk sitting perpendicular to him. From this sideways vantage point, he saw the man grab his thighs with his hands. Then the monk's abdominal muscles began to move. Three undulations to the right were followed by three to the left. The torso remained still and rigid. The monk rippled his stomach from top to bottom and finished off with violent shaking all over. Blake scanned the others. Now everyone raised himself off the ground and dropped like a stone. Blake watched incredulously as the whole sequence repeated three times. In the last round, the final bounce was higher and more powerful than anything that preceded it.

The monks sat perfectly still, and the lama said a few words. Steam began to rise from the monks' midsections. Soon vapor lifted from their shoulders, and copious amounts of water evaporated off the thin garments. Each monk, sitting in blissful peace, created his own cloud.

The lama approached Blake and guided him to his feet. *What's he doing?* Blake looked to Ang for guidance, but Ang said nothing. *I hope this guy doesn't think I'm going to drench my shirt and put it back on.* The lama took Blake to the adept he had been watching and said something to him. The young monk nodded and the lama forced Blake's hand down to feel the man's robe. *Dry! It's perfectly dry and warm!*

Blake pulled his hand away and rushed back to sit by Ang. Ang chuckled and leaned in. "It is tumo."

"Tumo?"

"Yes, it is a kind of yoga concerned with producing body heat."

Even as Ang explained what they were watching, the monks again rose and plunged their dry garments back into the frigid waters. They resumed their positions near their teacher. More Tibetan words followed. The adepts covered their bodies with the soaked repas and sat lotus style. Closing their eyes, they extended their arms and rested the palms up and open on their knees. Their breathing changed and Blake recognized them to be meditating. A few minutes passed. Blake saw water stream off the wet clothes and form puddles next to the monks, and still nothing happened. One monk rubbed his hands together and then his feet. Next to him, a couple of others did the same, until the whole group had accomplished this motion. Blake stared at the monk who initiated the sequence. The man exhaled loudly and shook in what appeared to be a thunderous burst of energy. Instantaneously, the whole repa shed water, forming a vapor cloud that rendered the monk all but invisible. One by one, the other monks disappeared in fog.

Had he not been there to witness these events, Blake would have thought the whole affair impossible. How could someone sit half-naked in the freezing cold and not exhibit physical effects? At no point did the adepts look cold or shiver. At no point had their skin shown the pink color of irritation or even the pale white of exposure. And how could their body heat dry the saturated garments? How did they do it?

Eventually, the clouds evaporated from the monks, and they sat in silence at their master's feet. Ang touched Blake on the shoulder and pointed back toward the monastery. The monks headed back to the winter stream, and Blake followed Ang back to the gompa.

"Are you going to tell me how they do that?" Blake said once they had moved away far enough not to be overheard.

Ang tented his hands as he walked, considering his response. "I am not altogether certain how it is done. It involves energy manipulation at a subtle level. Through yoga one learns to control breathing and that is the key to controlling mind and the subtle energies."

Blake threw up his hands, "Great, that's about as clear as mud!" He passed Ang and trudged back to the compound on his own. He retrieved his backpack, strode to the far end of the courtyard, and threw himself down on a step to one of the buildings. For once, he wanted to be on his own and away from Ang and all the odd things he had seen. He reached into his pack and grabbed his MP3 player, his only escape from this bizarre world he had been forced into. Closing his eyes, he let the music take him into familiar territory.

Chapter Twenty-Two

The next morning Blake found the gompa grounds coated in a light, airy snow. A quick storm had moved through during the night, leaving behind a low hanging sky, heavy with dark clouds. Voices, like water bubbling over rocks, drew him outside to find a group of monks seated chanting in an open space. Barefooted and wearing repas, the monks pursued their daily activities without noticing him. Today was going to be different though. Still frustrated by Ang's lack of knowledge and explanation, Blake decided to do his own investigation. No longer would he sit on the sidelines merely watching one incredible feat after another.

The mournful cry of a long trumpet interrupted the praying monks. They rose and gathered exactly the way they had done the previous day. Blake shivered, waiting for their teacher to arrive. *Today is even colder than yesterday. Well, I don't have to stay for the entire session. I just want a few answers and I'll be back in the warm monastery kitchen before long.*

The lama from the previous day's exercises appeared in the courtyard and ushered his pupils toward the mountain stream. Blake followed the group down to the water's edge. Thin ice glinted from the periphery of the running water, affirming the day's chill. The lama muttered a few undecipherable words, and the adepts went to the stream. The tinkling sound of ice cracking as they submerged their garments unnerved Blake for a moment. He had a plan, but he hesitated. *I can do this. If they can do it, I can at least try.* From under his jacket, Blake pulled out a folded repa he had borrowed from a storage cabinet inside the main gompa building. *I'm only borrowing it.*

Blake plunged the garment into the water and felt a shock from the cold travel up his arms, draining his body's heat. The adepts had already wrung out their repas and returned to their places. Blake struggled to wring the icy water out of his robe, but already his fingers were numb. He looked at the instructor, who wrinkled his brow and regarded him with curiosity. With the garment still dripping, Blake raced back to the others and stripped off his zipped parka. The students, clothed in their wet garments, were seated, waiting for their teacher. Blake slung his repa on over his cotton T-shirt and dropped to the ground. The force of the drop mitigated the sting of the cold to his upper torso.

Within seconds of sitting on the hard, frigid ground, Blake felt his teeth begin to chatter. Water ran down his chest and back, stabbing him with icy daggers. He started to shiver. The monks grabbed their thighs, and Blake copied the movement, trying with all his might to concentrate on what the adepts were doing. As he looked to his right, he saw a monk begin to work his stomach muscles. Three undulations right, then three undulations left. Blake attempted it but found his muscles didn't want to cooperate. He became increasingly agitated while he tried to emulate the movements. They had seemed so easy when he watched the previous day. A slight breeze from the direction of the water rippled his pants, and his repa started to crystallize and cling to his skin. As Blake watched with fascination and horror, the monks around him completed their tumo sequences and began to generate heat. Clouds rose to both sides of him. Cold and pale with clicking teeth, Blake's breathing slowed. Panic grasped him as he struggled to get up, but his legs would not move. He felt numb, cold, and weak. So weak. He tried to call out, but his voice produced only slurred monosyllables. The cold faded, and what he wanted more than anything was to take a nap. He rolled onto his right side and closed his eyes.

Blake felt his body being lifted by strong, caring arms. He remembered how his dad had waited up for him and carried him to bed when he was young. Then, like now, he wasn't fully conscious, but he'd always been comforted by the motion. Blake tried to rouse himself to see who had lifted him, but the pull of sleep overwhelmed him.

Slung into a chair like a sack of potatoes, Blake jerked awake and found himself in the monastery kitchen. The burly monk who ran the kitchen skidded the chair across the floor and toward the fire. The tumo instructor stood near the door with crossed arms and an irritated look. Blake's jacket and wet repa were removed as a couple of the adepts charged in with blankets. They took up positions at Blake's feet and began rubbing his body frantically. They bent his weak limbs, trying to stir the life force back into them. They stretched his hands and feet close to the fire. Blake attempted a few words, but still he didn't have the muscle control he needed for speech. Slowly, he felt his extremities begin to tingle. He bent his own fingers and stretched his own toes. The monks withdrew to stand by their master, far from the fire. Blake rubbed his hands together. "What happened?" he asked.

The burly monk forced a cup of hot Tibetan tea into his hands and smiled.

Ang burst into the room and went immediately to Blake's side. "Are you all right?"

Some of the tea dribbled down Blake's face. "I think so."

Ang pulled a blanket tightly around Blake and held it there like a hug. After a few moments, he left Blake to talk with the lama. They exchanged calm words near the door, and Blake saw the tumo practitioners and their teacher exit out the back door.

Returning to Blake's side, Ang refilled the tea cup. "The lama has told me you attempted to generate heat without the proper training. Is that so?"

Blake nodded, his head held down. "It didn't look hard. Yesterday, I watched them and I thought I could do it. So today, I followed them and tried it."

"Humm. It is harder than it looks." Ang readjusted the blanket that had slipped from Blake's shoulder.

"Ang, I've gone along with your decisions and I've seen some wild things. I'm tired of being a spectator. I'm tired of not knowing what's right or wrong, what's real and what isn't. This time I wanted to know, for sure. If I could do it, I could understand it. It would be real and I'd know it."

Ang knelt by Blake. "I understand. However, it was ill advised. Do you think I tried to climb just because I saw that others could do it? I did not purchase gear and take on Chomolungma. It took years of training, of learning, of imagining, before I ever attempted climbing. My being able to do it did not make it real."

Blake lifted his head and looked deeply into Ang's eyes. From those brown Sherpa eyes came an acceptance and an understanding between two men. Blake felt humbled by the compassionate response he received from Ang. His father would probably have yelled, or perhaps he would have launched into an exhaustive analysis of what could have happened. Ang didn't do that.

"I will go get you some dry clothes."

"Thanks. Ang, how long does it take to learn tumo?"

Ang ruffled his brow, searching for the information. "Three years, three months, and three days."

Blake chuckled. "You're making that up!"

Over the next week, Blake stayed on the grounds of the monastery. Not once did he stray down to the glacial stream, although he watched every day when the tumo teacher led his pupils out of the courtyard. He knew Ang was right. He didn't have to experience heat generation to know the monks were perfecting something down there. Ang had taken to doing odd jobs around the gompa, leaving Blake plenty of time to explore and watch the monks at work.

One afternoon Blake sat in the courtyard alone. The adepts proceeded on schedule to the stream while he stayed behind, soaking in the warm Himalayan sun. The journey with Ang had led him into a world that was so strange and so different from anything he had ever known. He ran his hand threw his hair and noticed how long it had become. His sense of time had been so disrupted by the queerness of traveling that he really didn't know what the date was or how long they had been on the road. Across the courtyard, Ang emerged from one of the buildings. Blake ran down the walkway to catch up with his friend.

"Ang, what's the date?" Blake asked.

Ang pulled his jacket sleeve up and checked his watch. "It is May 8th."

Together, the two walked toward the main hall.

"We've been on the road so long, I lost track. What day of the week is it?"

"It is Monday." Ang continued, "I have finished my work for the day, and I thought we could do some exploring on the hillside beyond the stream. What do you think?"

"That sounds great!"

"Good. I want to bring my pack, so you wait here and I will come back soon."

Blake nodded and resumed his seat overlooking the courtyard. A few minutes later, Ang joined him, carrying a small pack on his back.

As they headed toward the stream, Blake asked, "Do you know the trail?"

"No. It will be our adventure. Only for a few hours though, because cook has a particularly good guthuk, a stew of yak, that I do not care to miss."

They passed the stream where the monks sat in dry robes, meditating. Today the master seemed to be giving new instructions. Blake felt grateful for the beautiful, warm spring day that would guide their afternoon trek. In a shallow area of the stream, flat stones allowed Blake and Ang to cross the water in safety. The ground rose sharply on the other side. Ang led them along a well-trodden path paralleling the stream.

"Blake, I have been wondering if you have given consideration to what you have seen and how your yeti photos might affect others."

"I'm not sure what you mean," Blake replied.

Ang stopped and his eyes met Blake's. "You have seen many things now. Some of those I am certain you were meant to see."

"Yeah..."

Ang frowned. "If you decide to take the pictures back home and they are published in newspapers and on television, have you thought about what might happen to this land?"

"This land? No. What could happen?"

"That is not for me to say. I do not know your world. These are, perhaps, the issues the Rinpoche wants you to consider fully."

Blake drew in a deep breath through his nose and considered the possibility. Ang turned his attention back to the trail and they walked on in silence.

Blake recalled the sense of excitement he had when he first held the yeti photos. He remembered thinking that he held the solution to a mystery that had baffled people for centuries and his next thought had been that he wanted to share that knowledge. What good was knowing the solution to a secret when you're the only one who knows? The real exhilaration of the find lay in the anticipation that he would be able to tell others. Clearly, the Rinpoche and Ang didn't want that. Why not? What could happen?

Initially, the media would pick up the story. There would be interviews and lots of publicity. Maybe he'd get to go on TV and explain how he found the photos. There would be some money, but how much was hard to say. The rights to the photos could be sold, and he could charge for interviews. Who knew how much money might come to him? Didn't he deserve something? He had found the photos, and he had endured the trip that the Rinpoche required to get them back. Dad would insist that he put the money away for college, and that would be okay too, since it wasn't really about the money anyway.

Then, aside from sharing the secret, what was it about?

Maybe he hoped that disclosing the information would make him impossible to ignore anymore. Dad would have to notice a son whom the world paid attention to. Overnight he could become even more famous than some of the climbers who succeeded in climbing the world's highest peaks. But that wasn't what Ang had asked. Ang wanted to know how it might affect "this land." That would require some concentrated effort, and Blake decided to put the matter off until he could be alone to really think. Today he just wanted to have some fun exploring. There would be plenty of time for quiet contemplation.

Gradually, the trail grew steeper, and Blake felt his calf muscles tingle as they climbed. Although none of the ground around the monastery had been lush, there at least had been low lying shrubs. Here the terrain turned dusty and barren. After a while, Blake's throat burned in the thin, dry air. They crested a hillside peak and could look across the way to a flat plateau. Separated by a plummeting gorge, the plateau sat slightly higher than the ground where Blake and Ang stood. Atop this desolate outcropping, three men were busy at work.

"Let me borrow your binoculars! I see people over there," Blake exclaimed. Ang squinted to see the familiar brown chubas rippling in the breeze. "Ah, we have found them. Let us sit." He squatted, quickly produced the binoculars, and handed them to Blake.

Blake raised the glasses and asked, "Found who?"

"The rogyapas. The body cutters. Several days ago the astrologer at the gompa was consulted on the death of a villager. This date was determined to be auspicious for sky burial."

Spinning the center wheel of the binoculars brought the sight into focus. Three men dressed in simple brown robes moved around a body wrapped in a similar homespun cloth. Blake tried to view the corpse's face, but the angle of the body didn't allow it.

"So you brought me to a funeral?" Blake asked passively. *Why did he think I should see this? Believe me, I've been to enough funerals lately.*

Ang rubbed his chin. "Precisely. In your world, there is ground burial. Tibetans have four kinds of burial respecting the four elements—air, water, fire, and earth. Sky burial is used at higher altitudes where the ground cannot be broken and there is a scarcity of wood. In other places, ground burial, water burial, and cremation might be used. It is sky burial that has special significance for us."

Through the binoculars, Blake watched as a monk in burgundy stepped out from behind a huge boulder and positioned himself near the corpse. "They're taking the robe off the body. It's a man. Now the monk is marking something on the chest and stomach. Ang, do you want to see this?"

"No, you can describe what you see for me."

The other men unfolded large knives that flashed in the midday sun. Blake recoiled but didn't look away. "Holy...! Now they have knives out. What are they going to do?"

One of the rogyapas sliced across the corpse's chest, making a deep incision. The other man, brandishing his weapon, advanced on the body. With forceful precision, the two men worked at cutting and removing intact body organs. A pile of body parts began to grow near the men. Blake looked on in fascinated horror, but after a few moments, he felt guilty about watching the scene. He let the binoculars drop to his chest.

Gulping air, he said, "It's pretty gruesome. I guess you've seen it before."

Ang went to Blake's side and took the glasses. He assumed Blake's role. "Now flesh is removed from bone. The rogyapas have their mallets in hand. They smash the bones."

Blake's stomach lurched. He could hear the pounding echo of shattering bone through the mountain passes. As if that was a special signal, vultures appeared, circling in the sky overhead. At first they flew in high, wide circles, catching an updraft, but eventually the ominous black birds dropped lower and homed in on the corpse's location. One of the birds dropped to the ground but was chased off by one of the men, who wildly swung a rope.

Ang continued, "Bone is mixed with barley flour."

Swaying slightly with the realization of what was happening, Blake said, "The vultures eat the body..." Even as he said it, more vultures arrived to join those already circling. Blake and Ang found themselves in shadows as the huge birds flew directly over them. *Sick. So sick. So uncivilized. At least we had the decency to bury my grandfather.*

Even without the binoculars, Blake could see two of the workers cast body parts onto a high, flat rock. The other man still flung the rope, keeping the vultures away. Eventually he let the rope drop. The ebony birds instantaneously dropped from the sky.

Ang handed the glasses back to Blake. Against his better judgment, but caught up in the moment, Blake peered through them.

The vultures lunged and ripped the pieces apart with no regard for it being a human body. Then it occurred to Blake that to the birds, it was just food. Food that had been prepared especially for them and would sustain them in the coming days. One life was gone, but other lives carried on in this inhospitable place. It took only a few minutes for the ravenous vultures to consume their grizzly meal. A loud crashing sound drew Blake's attention back to the workers. They smashed the deceased man's skull with a large club, gathered the remains, and fed it to the birds.

Blake sank down next to Ang. "I'm sure you wanted me to see this for a reason. I mean, you must have had more in mind than giving me nightmares. At least, I hope so. And—I can't rule out the nightmares."

Ang's eyes flickered with excitement, and he cuffed Blake playfully on the shoulder. "True. How true. Sky burial reminds us of the impermanence of life and the certainty of death. No matter who we are, what we acquire, or how we live; we all come to the same end. Death walks with us each day, every day."

Blake nodded, his face twisted into a knowing frown. "What about the vultures? At first, I was shocked by seeing them eating human flesh, and then I thought about that saying 'life goes on.' The man was dead and nothing was going to change that. Why not let the living benefit, if it's possible?"

"Sustenance for the birds is the final generous gift given by the deceased. Death gives life."

They sat together, silently, for a long time. As Blake watched the vultures consume their remaining meal, he grew comfortable in the idea that life and death were intertwined in an inevitable dance. Eventually, understanding supplanted horror.

When it was all over, the monk and the rogyapas gathered their tools and left the high plateau. The vultures took to the air and circled. Soon they were gone as well. Blake looked at Ang. "It's done. The man's body is gone and now the family has only its memories. Would the man have reincarnated yet?"

Ang leaned forward and ruffled Blake's long dark hair. "You are asking good questions, and I promise to answer. Tomorrow we will set out on our last trek before heading back to Tengboche. Then, I will answer your inquiries. Now we must get back for cook's guthuk."

"I hope no one's insulted if I skip eating tonight. I really don't have an appetite."

"Do not fear, you will be hungry by the time we hike back. These feelings will fade and your body will seek food."

"If you say so." Blake rose and hoisted Ang's day pack onto his back.

Chapter Twenty-Three

By the time Blake crossed the stream near the gompa, his stomach growled. Even after the upsetting images he had seen that afternoon, his body still required nourishment. Ang plowed forward in front of him, never showing any sign of slowing down. Blake felt winded and fell several yards behind the Sherpa. In the monastery's courtyard, he dumped the pack and sat down hard on a doorway step. Ang waved and disappeared into the kitchen.

Ang emerged carrying two steaming bowls. Behind him, a young boy carried a teapot and cups. Ang handed Blake a bowl and lowered his face to draw in the meal's aroma. "Ahh. This is just what I wanted," he said. He thrust his spoon into the mixture and gulped down some of the savory stew.

The young boy waited patiently as Ang and Blake settled themselves on the steps. Carefully, the boy placed the tea and cups between them and retreated. "Thanks!" Blake called out. The boy shuffled back to the kitchen.

Blake tasted the mixture and knew why Ang liked it so much. It was spicier than the usual stews they had eaten, and although Blake couldn't identify all the ingredients, he ate it happily. Pouring the tea, he asked, "So where are we going tomorrow?"

"The next leg of our journey will take us into the high country where we will camp. It is the most remote of locations and will allow us to experience the land without interruption. After that, we go back to see the Rinpoche."

Blake sipped the strong tea. "Is this where I'm supposed to think about 'the land'?"

"It is my sincere hope that you will do that. Perhaps you will allow me to aid in this process. At gompa, debate was my strength."

"So you want to help me come to the right decision?"

Ang shook his head. "No. I do not know what is best. Through talk, we may find an agreeable answer. If you do not want my help, I will not give it. However, if there is a time when discussion is necessary, I offer myself."

Blake nodded. He knew Ang wanted to leave life at the gompa behind so he could consider the question of the photographs. Without the comfort of known surroundings, he would have to confront what releasing the photographs might do to the region.

Ang shook Blake awake in the darkness of their small cubicle. The lighting of several butter lamps cast an eerie, flickering glow in the room. The shuffling of feet through the corridor indicated that morning life at the gompa was underway. Blake shook his head as he drew himself up into a sitting position. He wondered if he could do the same things day in, day out for years on end. A monk's life was governed by routine. Some boys left their families at seven or eight, like Ang had done.

Blake doubted he could live that way. The trip to the Himalayas had whetted his appetite for travel and adventure, and he vowed not to stay trapped in that small town in Ohio. *That might be all right for Mom, but not for me. Maybe I'm more like Dad when it comes to new things. He seems to crave them.*

Blake and Ang quickly stowed their gear and headed out to the kitchen. They downed some nearly tasteless, gray barley gruel. The steel color of the morning began to lift as they hit the trail. They retraced their steps from the previous afternoon, following the stream and ending up close to where the sky burial had been performed. Today, no vultures flew overhead.

A brilliant sun emerged against a clear blue sky. Blake enjoyed the trek. He inhaled fresh mountain air and relaxed as his body fell into its rhythm. They followed the fast moving stream as it twisted its way north. Dwarf willow trees grew in clusters at the water's edge. Blake snapped off a small branch and inhaled its musky greenery. Life persisted in small ways even in this high, arid zone.

After a couple of hours' walking, they stopped for their first break. Blake downed water while Ang sat back and closed his eyes. He removed a brown strand of beads from his pocket. His lips moved, and his fingers slid over the beads. After one circuit around the beads, Ang's eyes popped open.

Blake recapped his water bottle. "Yesterday you promised to tell me about what happens after death."

"I did." Ang dropped the rosary back into his pocket and straightened up, looking into Blake's eyes. "First, I must explain that you and I probably view the moment of death differently. Let us begin there. In your culture, how do you define death?"

Blake sighed. *Here we go. We're having a debate already. Why can't he just answer my questions?* "Death is when the body dies. There is no brain activity or heartbeat."

A spark flashed in Ang's eyes and he sat forward. "Here is the difference. Buddhists see death arise with the appearance of the mind of clear light. Death is a process, not a solitary event. For three days after your idea of death, consciousness remains with the body. Any disturbance, like burial or cremation, could result in negative influences and possibly lower rebirth. That is why the death of the man whom we saw undergo sky burial must have occurred at least three days before the event we witnessed."

"That's weird. You mean that after someone dies physically, there is some part of them that's still aware? Still in the body?"

Ang squinted and tented his hands. "Essentially so. This consciousness then passes into a temporary state called bardo. A person could be in bardo for as little as seven days or up to forty nine days looking for a suitable life situation. The reincarnation is governed by the karma of the past life."

Blake was familiar with the term *karma*. Slade always talked about his karma. Usually Slade's references were tied to unfortunate events in his life, things he had no control over. At those times, he'd say, "Man, my karma sucks!"

"What's bardo like and what is its purpose? Why aren't people reincarnated right away?" Blake asked.

"Bardo can be disorienting and scary for an unprepared person. It can be loud, with bright lights, and the appearance of deities. Most people rush back to the comforts of cyclic existence without fully realizing what they are doing. With that comfort comes the desire and pain of life. Those fully prepared for death, usually yogins, can bypass bardo and become buddhas. Time in bardo is spent searching for an appropriate place to be reborn."

"And I might not be human the next time around?"

"Correct. A human life is very rare and very precious. Rebirth into another realm is always possible."

Blake unscrewed his water bottle and considered the idea of "another realm". "So if I'm bad in this life, I can come back as a pig?" He chuckled, then sipped his water.

"Perhaps. But there are other realms as well. You know of the human and animal realms. There are four others: the Hell Realm, the Hungry Ghost Realm, the Demigod Realm, and the God Realm."

Blake brushed his hair from his face. "That's a lot of choices." They sat quietly for a few moments, Blake digesting the new information. He supposed he should ask about the Hell and Hungry Ghost realms, but they sounded so obviously unpleasant that he thought it better to leave well enough alone.

Back on the trail, they continued to follow the mountain stream. Gradually the path meandered off, growing rockier and less defined, with rough scrub bushes lining one side.

With Ang in the lead, Blake called out, "How long have you known my dad?"

As Ang turned around, the momentum shifted his weight and caused him to slip on a sharp rock. Flailing to stay upright, he reached out and grabbed at the sparse vegetation.

"Aiyeeee." Ang found his footing and pulled his hand from the bush, dripping blood.

Blake rushed to Ang. A two-inch laceration bled profusely as Ang dropped his pack to the ground.

"I'll get the medical supplies. You hold that up and put some pressure on it," Blake commanded.

A grin broke across Ang's face and he let Blake take over. Ang held his hand up and applied pressure. Blake carefully spread the supplies on the ground noting the inventory. As he ripped open a disinfecting wipe, he asked, "Is it still bleeding?"

"Not so much," Ang said.

"Good. Let's get it cleaned up and wrapped." Blake washed the cut and applied a piece of sterile gauze. He wrapped the wound with self-sticking tape, tight enough to keep it from reopening but loose enough for Ang to move his hand.

"Good. Thank you," Ang said, inspecting the work.

Blake dropped the kit into Ang's pack. "No problem, just don't grab any more branches!"

They continued along, paying very close attention to the uneven rocks strewn along the trail. Eventually, the walkway went back to being dusty, compressed earth. Blake came up alongside Ang.

"You wanted to know how long I have known your father," Ang said.

Blake nodded.

"I met him last year when he did some trekking. It was before the climbing season, and I was one of the guides. I liked him right away. Always ready to help."

"I guess I knew it had to have been from then. I remember when he left last spring. It seemed like he wanted to get away from me and Mom more than he wanted to go on the trip. When he came back, he said he had "gotten his head together." Within days, my parents were getting divorced."

Ang looked at him and waited for more. Feeling Ang's eyes, Blake walked on in silence.

"You seem to have your father's gift for healing," Ang said, raising his injured hand.

"Me? No. I don't want to be a doctor."

"Last year, I had a man fall and break a leg along a remote trail. Your father splinted it and practically carried the man off the mountain."

Blake nodded. He had heard the story before. "I know he's a good doctor."

"But not a good man?" Ang said quietly.

"Humpf, maybe just not a good dad."

"Perhaps things will change. Do you want that?"

"Sure, but I don't think it's likely. I thought that if I came out here and spent time with him, things might. But as you can see, I'm here and he's not. I'm getting used to it," Blake said. *How can I explain to Ang that Dad's just not interested in having a son? Everything else and everybody else comes before me.*

Chapter Twenty-Four

Ahead lay a mountain chiseled in rock. A narrow trail ran gouged into its side a couple of hundred feet up. Ang pointed. "We go there!" Blake looked at the rock face with its mottled browns. The incline wasn't too steep, but it would give them a workout.

"How much farther?" Blake asked.

"Another hour or so."

The cheese and bread they had eaten for lunch sat heavily in Blake's stomach. As they mounted the trail, he felt protected by the mountain on one side and the huge rippling of rock on the other. Soon Blake perspired under the late-afternoon sun. He opened his jacket and stuffed his hat into his pocket while he struggled to keep up with Ang, who seemed to bounce up the trail. Mares' tail clouds floated peacefully overhead, framing their journey.

In the quiet, Blake's thoughts drifted back to his dad. Ang had a point. Once all this was over and he met up with Dad in Katmandu, maybe the two of them could spend some time together and really talk. Maybe there would be time. Possibly, a couple of days in the Nepalese capital could do the trick. He and Dad alone. What would he say then, if he had the opportunity?

He'd tell him how hard the divorce had really been. Teased unmercifully in the small town, he'd known no relief until he'd met Slade. He knew some things about Mom now. He wanted to know why no one had told him about her *boyfriend*. Was there anything else Dad knew that he had a right to know, too? So many things to talk about.

Blake sighed as the realization of his self-centeredness hit him. He would tell Dad about his feelings and about Mom's grief, but he also knew he had to find out how Dad coped with it all. Did he have regrets? How did the divorce affect him? Did he run away from the pain by going to the Himalayas to escape everything?

Up ahead, Ang stopped and looked up. Something must have caught his eye. He looked at Blake and put his index finger to his mouth, indicating silence. His hand motioned Blake forward slowly. Once at Ang's side, Blake scanned the rough mountainside but saw nothing. Sherpa eyes were apparently as good as a hawk's. Blake shook his head, bewildered, and Ang pointed to an area of rock less than a hundred feet away. Still, Blake saw nothing but a sea of grays. A quick blur of motion drew his eye to a small region of the rock. He gazed intently. Another quick, snapping sweep of something and Blake's eyes focused on a thick, black-and-gray spotted vine.

"Snow leopard," Ang whispered.

Blake followed the tail up and found the large cat, almost perfectly camouflaged against a rock outcropping. "Binoculars?" he mouthed.

Ever so slowly, Ang eased the pack off his back and handed it to Blake. Blake unzipped it and extracted the glasses while keeping his eyes on the cat. Cautiously, he raised the binoculars and adjusted the focus.

The view startled him at first. The ghostly gray-and-white feline stared at him with its pale green eyes. Powerfully built for life in the high mountains, the cat sat in repose, watching the valley below. Blake saw the animal's black spots and rosettes, and he understood more fully how the leopard blended in so well.

Suddenly, the cat whipped its head around, looking across and above where Blake and Ang stood. Blake dropped the binoculars and followed the leopard's gaze. On that hillside a few gowa, Tibetan gazelle, nervously grazed. By the time Blake looked back toward the cat, it had moved forward, crouching low. It hopped down, padded feet hitting boulders, advancing on its prey. Unaware of the leopard's presence, the gazelle spread out over the hillside. The cat settled only yards away from one of them. It waited, hidden amongst the rocks. Blake watched, captivated, as the gazelle approached the hungry feline, totally unaware of the invisible threat.

In an instant, the cat sprang, closing the distance between the two animals. The gazelle leaped down, narrowly escaping the flying feline's first move. The cat hit the ground, spun, and used its massive tail to right itself. The power of the motion dislodged several large rocks that hurtled toward the valley floor. The rocks crashed into others, flinging a mini-avalanche toward Blake and Ang.

"Look out!" Blake screamed as he threw himself out of the path of the oncoming assault.

Ang jumped in the opposite direction. One foot caught on a nearby stone and he stumbled, falling and slipping over the side of the trail. The avalanche crashed between them, and Blake rushed to where he'd seen Ang disappear.

"Ang!" he called, sliding to the edge. "Ang! Are you okay?" Dropping to his knees, Blake looked down the smooth drop-off. Fifty feet or so below, perched on a narrow ledge, Ang pulled himself to his feet. Beneath him, huge boulders prevented any escape downward.

"I am all right!" Ang yelled back.

Blake looked at the tilted, smooth rock face that Ang slid down before coming to rest on the ledge. He was safe from falling and miraculously unhurt. They had been very lucky. With a good amount of rope, Ang could be easily rescued.

"Hang on! I'm going to get some rope." Blake dug in Ang's pack and found the climbing line. He wrapped one end around a huge boulder and tied it securely.

Extending the rope, he kneeled and cast the other end to Ang.

"Here it comes!"

The coiled rope hit the incline and fell open, cascading downward. Gravity pulled it straight and taut. Blake gasped. At least fifteen feet too short, the line dangled, useless. He jumped to his feet and ran back to inspect the rope tied to the boulder. Even if he untied it and secured it to himself standing near the edge of the cliff, the line still would not reach Ang.

Back at the edge, Blake scanned the boulders near Ang, checking to see if anything could be piled up to help Ang get to the rope.

"Ang, can you move any of the rocks to give yourself a boost?"

"No. There is nothing. Everything is huge. Are you carrying any rope in your pack?"

"No, nothing like that."

Blake pushed his unruly mass of hair from his face and drummed his finger on his lower lip. He felt a wave of nausea rise as he struggled against fear. Alone, out in the middle of nowhere, with no resources. What could he do? His thoughts of despair piled one on top of the other. This was serious. Ang could die. He would never find his way out alone. His vision blurred, and he felt disoriented from hanging over the edge. Vomit rose in his throat. He spat it aside and suddenly felt very hot. He pulled back away from the cliff and sat in a heap, shaking.

"Blake," Ang called.

Don't panic!

Blake forced himself back to the drop-off, this time resting on his belly.

"I'm here!"

"The place we were going is less than an hour away. A few seasons ago, I stashed extra gear in one of the caves for emergencies. This is such an occasion. You must go and retrieve it and come back."

"By myself? What if I can't find it?"

"I will give you expert instructions. Do you have paper to make a map?"

"Hold on, I'll get something."

Blake tore open his pack and ripped a page from a book. With pencil in hand, he yelled down, "Okay, go ahead."

"You will follow this trail east. The sun will be behind you."

"Okay, go slow. I'm writing everything down."

Blake drew a horizontal line and put the sun overhead with an arrow pointing left. He marked E for east on the right side of the paper.

"From here the trail climbs and circles a steep valley. Stay on the path. The main trail is clearly marked. Do not let your mind wander, and do not deviate from the main trail. That is very important. After that, there is a sharp descent, and eventually, you will come to a rope bridge."

"All right. Wait while I put that all down." Blake scribbled more pictures and notes.

"The bridge should be fine, but watch your footing. Once you cross, you will descend into a narrow valley of limestone with many caves. In the second tier of caves and the second cave in, you will find the extra gear. Bring everything."

Blake pulled his sleeve back, glancing at his watch. "Okay. If it takes an hour to go and an hour to get back, then I should be here by four o'clock."

"Before you go, I want you to slide my water bottle and my silver blanket down. Wrap the bottle in the blanket, so that the weight will carry it."

"Right."

Blake retrieved the items and added a couple of energy bars from his own pack. Carefully, he tied the bundle together using his belt with the skull buckle. The Goth gear seemed outrageously ill-suited to provide Ang with the supplies that would sustain life. He hoped Ang wouldn't notice. At the edge, he gingerly lined the package up with his friend and let it go. The bundle skidded down the rock face and into Ang's outstretched hands.

"Thanks! Blake, be careful. Take your time. Do not travel at night. If you cannot make it back before nightfall, wait for morning. I will be fine here."

Blake rummaged through Ang's pack taking the medical kit, the flashlight, and the rest of the water. He stuffed those into his backpack and zipped it closed. Hoisting his pack up, he called to Ang, "I'll be back soon!"

"Yes, Blake. Take care!"

A quick glance at his crude drawing and Blake set off east. The first quarter mile or so seemed much like the trail he and Ang had already traversed. Slowly, the path grew steeper, and Blake's knees felt the strain. He moved quickly, not wanting Ang to have to stay on the ledge any longer than necessary. As the trail became more difficult, Blake forced himself to slow down and listen to his body. It would do no good to race along only to have an accident or lose his way. Above him and a good distance out in front, he spotted another group of gowa. What had happened to the snow leopard and its prey? Could the cat be sitting somewhere above him waiting to pounce?

How many Himalayan predators watched his every move? Ang had not mentioned any dangerous animals, but seeing the leopard convinced Blake there were others. Bears. There had to be bears. He'd read about them. Some people even believed that the yeti was one of several bears found in the region. He knew that was wrong. The Tibetan bear, the Tibetan black bear, the blue bear, the Isabelle bear, and the panda all lived here

Into The Land of Snows | 177

somewhere. Blake remembered the panda he'd seen in the National Zoo. The enormous black-and-white creature slept while he watched. The bamboo-eating bear couldn't be much of a threat. Besides, bamboo didn't grow up this high. So—no food, no bear. But what about the others? If the snow leopard could hunt antelope and survive, then maybe some of the other bears could do that too. Logically, Blake concluded that bears were possible and so were yetis. He'd keep alert for any signs of them.

He tried to remember the safety rules for being out hiking. In California, anyone who hiked knew to look out for cougars and bears. This was the same thing, just like home. *For bears, I need to make a lot of noise. This alerts the bear that someone is around, and that way, I'm not likely to surprise the animal.* Blake scuffed his boots and kicked at random rocks along the path. *If I encounter a bear, I should back away slowly and never, never run. If attacked, curl into a ball...or climb a tree?*

Blake paused and leaned against the mountain. He looked behind him and above him, checking for motion or shadows where bears might hide. Nothing. Could they camouflage themselves like the leopard had? He used his hand to push himself away from the rock face and felt a rippled texture beneath his palm. His fingers moved over the lines and he realized it was a carving. Tibetan letters lined up, spelling out a prayer. Blake took comfort in the creation, knowing that others had passed this way before him. He said, "Om mani padme hum." Saying the only mantra he knew couldn't hurt.

Blake smiled and moved on. *I hope the carving didn't say "so and so-killed by a bear on this trail...."* The smile morphed into a smirk. *"So and so killed by a yeti..."*

The trail narrowed until Blake could just squeeze his body through. He turned to check behind him, and the pack became wedged between the rocks. Lodged in sideways, he swung himself in the opposite direction and had a fleeting thought about a story on himalayannews.com. Something about a trekker dying on a little-known trail when his pack became hopelessly stuck. Poor guy forgot he could slip the pack off. Panic and altitude created an amazing number of ways to die out alone in the mountains. Luckily, the pack popped free, and there would be no news story of an unlucky trekker from Ohio.

Blake pushed forward, noting the afternoon storm clouds that meandered in the distance. *What I really don't need is a weather complication.* He wondered what Ang would do on the mountainside alone. Was he sitting, just waiting, or praying? *He'll be all right. He's a Sherpa. Over the years, he must have been in far worse situations. Probably seen a lot too.*

Rounding the side of the mountain, Blake shuddered at a sheer drop-off. Apparently the trail had been enclosed at one point, but now an open-sided ledge stood between him and the materials he needed to rescue Ang. Did a boulder crash down from above and take part of the mountain? Did the melting and refreezing of rock finally cleave off a huge chunk? With enough room to cross, Blake drew in an icy breath and told himself not to look down. He pushed himself against the rock face and took baby steps forward. Slowly, slowly he edged by the exposed trail.

On the other side of the danger, Blake quivered as he glanced back at the drop-off. A misstep there and he would have plunged hundreds of feet to his death. Ang would still be waiting on the ledge with no hope of rescue.

The wind picked up, blasting frigid air full force into Blake's exposed face. Sunglasses shielded his eyes, but the rest of his face stung with the onslaught. Heavy, dark clouds propelled by strong gusts headed toward him. The whole Himalayan region was known for its unpredictable weather. It could be warm and sunny one minute and snowing the next. Blake knew the reason Mount Everest was so dangerous was not that it was the highest mountain, but rather that fast-moving weather patterns often caught climbers unaware. Weather killed far more climbers than the mountain ever would. And here he stood directly in the path of a raging storm.

Blake struggled against the wind, putting one foot in front of the other, gasping to get a breath. Sometimes, he had to swing his head left just to breathe. The gusts eventually pushed so hard against him he could no longer fight it. He took refuge in a crevasse behind a boulder, pressed in tightly with his head facing the mountain. He clutched his arms to his chest, holding the pack straps, fearing every moment that the wind would rip his supplies off his back.

The storm intensified, throwing snow down on him and the valley below. His arms ached, but he feared shifting too much. He tried to relax, to tell himself that while these blizzards were violent, many of them fizzled quickly. He prayed this would be one of those fast-moving events.

The storm raged on, and still he huddled against the mountain. Occasionally, he tried to peek out from his hiding place to see if the weather was changing. He saw whiteout conditions the couple of times he looked over his shoulder. He quickly retreated to safety, noting the amount of snow that had blown in around and on top of him. If the storm didn't break soon, it wouldn't be long until he was buried in the springtime snow.

Staring at the gray rock inches from his face, Blake forced himself to remain calm and optimistic. He snickered as the wind roared. *If all this is an illusion, why would I create such a hell? Ang stuck on a ledge, me freezing in a freak snowstorm? If I were in control, I'd create a different illusion. First off, Ang wouldn't be stuck. We'd still be walking along together and it would be a sunny day, so warm we didn't even need jackets.*

The wind died and the snow stopped. Blake shook himself off and stepped out from his shelter into knee-deep snow. *How will I ever find the trail now?*

Chapter Twenty-Five

Blake shuffled along. Already his jeans were stiff and crusted with the newly fallen snow. Before the storm, he had realized that the trail had begun to descend. He carefully plodded his way down, searching for ground that looked level. With his pace so slow, he knew he'd never reach Ang by four o'clock. *What time is it?*

Rigid, gloved fingers scraped to uncover his watch. It was nearly five already. Blake's heart pounded. If he didn't find the rescue gear quickly, he might be forced to stay the night at the caves, and that would mean Ang would be stranded until the next morning. A night spent out, fully exposed in the high country, even in spring, could be difficult. *At least Ang has the blanket, food and water. With any luck, the storm missed him. Pray the snow missed him.*

As he pressed forward, he became more comfortable with the snow's presence. The strain of struggling in its depths had him perspiring, and he unzipped his jacket and mopped his brow with his glove. With a slight turn in the trail, the rope bridge came into focus. *It's not far now. I can do this, and Ang won't be left out tonight.*

That realization sent a rush of newfound energy coursing through his body. He descended more quickly, bracing himself on boulders, making his way to the bridge. As Ang had told him, the rope bridge spanned a small stream. It was hard to tell the condition of the bridge, as it hung ten feet above the water covered in snow. Blake shook the guide ropes, freeing a cascade of flakes that looked like powdered sugar sprinkled on a cake his grandmother would have served. The ropes appeared to be intact. Feeling the pressure of time, he raised himself up and onto the bridge. He kicked at the snow mound in front of him, revealing wooden planks. Rocking the structure side to side cleared away some of the snow. Blake crossed the bridge without hesitation.

On the other side stood a rough and rocky mountainside very much like the one he had just come from. He reached in his pocket to retrieve his map. Somewhere, not far from here, he should find the limestone caves. But where? The map didn't help. There was a marking for the bridge and the word "caves" next to it. What had Ang said? He racked his brain but couldn't recall any additional details.

Scanning the ground Blake could see a depression that, although snow covered, seemed to be a trail. The path ran around the side of the mountain, facing the stream and heading north. He followed it, and within minutes, he stood in a protected valley of golden sandstone. Farther along, he saw the rock face riddled with holes. The caves! *Second row, second cave in, is where I should find the gear.*

Blake raced to the cliff side, grateful to have found the caves finally. Wild animals and a blizzard were not going to keep him from rescuing Ang. He hoisted himself to the second level, bypassing the first row of caves. With more time, he would gladly have explored these abandoned spaces, but time was growing short. He pressed himself against the sandstone wall and slid by the first cave's opening. Looking behind him, he peered into its blackness. He couldn't see anything, so he moved to the next opening.

The entrance to the cave, barely four feet tall, required Blake to stoop to look inside. Again, he could not penetrate its darkness. He called out, "Hey, anybody home?" and felt the ridiculousness of the situation. Of course, no one answered. Duh.

A few moments of riffling through his pack allowed him to produce a flashlight. When shown into the darkness, a compact hand-carved space emerged. A clump of gear sat stowed at the back of the cave. He signed in relief and quickly ran the light around every inch of the compartment to make sure there were no surprises. With the cave safe, he made his way to the supplies.

Ang had left two kinds of climbing rope, crampons, various hardware, a medical kit, energy bars, and a couple of liters of water. Blake retrieved the mini survival station and then zipped his bulging pack. He glanced at his watch and noted the time was five-thirty. He still might be able to reach Ang. Rising to his feet, he heard the distant murmur of chanting.

Am I going crazy? He leaned forward, straining to hear the sounds. His efforts were rewarded with high-pitched singsong syllables that appeared to be coming from above. Blake swung his flashlight up, illuminating the ceiling of the cave. Quickly, he moved the light over its surface until the light fell on a hole in a back corner. Letting go of the backpack, he shuffled to the opening. The chanting grew louder and clearer. Tiny flickers of flame danced around the slot. Blake's heart leaped when he realized he was not alone. Ang thought the caves were abandoned, but now Blake knew some monk had taken up residence in the cave above him.

He cast his beam of light to the floor and ran from the cave, thrilled by the prospect of another human being so close. Outside, he glanced up, trying to decide which of the cave entrances held the monk. Blake briefly considered yelling for help, but he dismissed that idea. Now that he had found the gear, the situation was no longer so desperate. Obviously, deep in prayer, no monk would want to be disturbed by the shouting of a stranger. Far better to seek the man out and ask politely for assistance. Not that he needed much help now, but perhaps the company of another person just to walk with him back to Ang would be beneficial.

Two caves looked promising. Positioned above, but in line with the cave he had just exited, the first cave sat at least ten feet off the ground. The other cave, while lower on the cliff face, didn't appear to line up correctly. Blake felt confident the monk resided in the higher of the two. He saw toeholds in the dry, soft sandstone and proceeded to climb. About halfway up, a narrow ledge ran to the other cave Blake had already dismissed.

The sun had begun to sink, casting the valley into an ominous place of shadows. Ang would be spending the night alone, trapped until Blake could make it back to him. The sudden loss of light sent a chill down Blake's back as he struggled higher. Finally, he pulled himself up and over the edge. He sat huddled before the dark cave. Silence. He flashed his light into the space and found the cave to be even smaller than the one below.

He rose and shouted, "Anybody here?" No answer. He would have to explore the other cave lower down.

Blake eased himself over the edge, feeling for a toehold. His fingers dug into the gritty rock and his right foot found safety as he moved down. At the ledge, he scurried to the next cave. The entranceway was large enough that Blake didn't need to duck. Stepping through, he snapped the flashlight on and found himself in a huge, carefully constructed chamber. It was at least twenty by twenty square feet, and Blake saw how much the cave looked like the interior of a room at a monastery. Thick wooden beams, painted red, spanned the ceiling. Decorative columns, like those he had seen in outdoor courtyards, seemed to prop the whole space up. The walls were covered in paintings of deities and bodhisattvas. Blake hurried to the center of the room, still wondering if he had found the right place. No mantras greeted him, and no monk was present.

On a far wall, the image of one of the deities appeared to be cut in half. Blake approached to investigate and found the rest of the image hidden behind a wall that ran perpendicular to the painting. This passageway led out of the chamber. With his light held in front, Blake slipped down the tight walkway. After a few steps he began to hear the chanting again. *I'm in the right spot!* He jogged the last few yards with the mantras growing louder. He rounded a corner and halted.

A small, dark cavity, illuminated with butter lamps, opened before him. A lone monk dressed in burgundy sat cross-legged with his back to Blake. He watched the holy man sway slightly, deep in trance. The warble of his voice echoed hauntingly.

Blake watched silently for some moments before approaching. Standing near the man's right shoulder afforded him a good view of the sand mandala on the floor in front of the adept. Tight concentric rings enclosed a series of rectangles. From their midpoints radiated stacked rectangular shapes resembling stupas. The center of the design contained more circles, and inside those were brightly colored flower petals. Small, intricate orbs of many colors floated between the stupas.

Blake had seen these traditional works in books but had never seen an actual one until now. The complex geometric design must have taken weeks or perhaps months for the monk to complete on his own. Each grain of colored sand was delivered individually using a tapered copper tube. Sand in yellow, green, red, white, blue, and black rested in bowls against a wall. Understanding the amount of work involved in creating the sand mandala, Blake hung back out of respect, not wanting to interrupt the ritual.

The monk's voice deepened, bouncing ominous rhythms off the walls. Blake took several steps back. After repeating the dark chants, the man's voice rose to a high singsong pitch and then became silent. *Should I let him know I'm here now?*

A white, ethereal smoke materialized at the center of the mandala. Thin at first, it resembled a smoker's exhalation. Blake held his position but leaned in to get a better look. As it swirled, the puff became denser. It rose and spread out, filling the space over the design. Contained by the mandala, it spun faster and faster, becoming thicker and whiter. Not a grain of sand was displaced by the powerful whirlwind. Blake took several steps back, unsure what would follow. Butterflies sprang to life in his gut, but his sense of curiosity held him rooted in position.

Fed by unseen energy, the tornado cloud now pulsed with color. Yellow popped to green, to blue, and then to red. All the colors mixed to form a reddish brown. The gaseous haze now seemed to solidify, taking form. *Making something!* A quick glance at the monk revealed him still in trance, eyes staring, fixed on his creation.

A hulking man-sized shape started to resolve from the vapor, hanging as an outline in the air. Blake shivered at the conjured image. *What was this thing?* The spinning slowed, and the body gained distinct appendages. Wispy arms reached forward. Legs, bent at the knees, stretched toward the floor, hovering above the sand painting.

Blake gasped, cupping his mouth in his hand. All over the creature, flowing red hair emerged as the body continued to solidify. The creature was still slightly translucent above the shoulders. Blake watched wide-eyed. A brown cloud near the head slowed, losing its power. Red hair sprouted crazily from the entity's head. Within seconds, the face of mih teh materialized, and Blake recognized the creature from Mallory's photos. A dark, bald face with penetrating brown eyes looked beyond the monk.

Yeti, a conjured creature, an illusion!

Saying that in his head broke the terror Blake had felt. The awareness that the entity before him had been a creation of the mind, something like a mirage, or a trick by an experienced magician, calmed him. The creature had no power and couldn't hurt him. The monk wasn't in danger. Soon the mirage would evaporate back into the thin atmosphere and everything would return to normal.

Suspended over the mandala, mih teh floated, frozen in space. Blake relaxed and started to enjoy the event as if it were a magic show. The monk remained in an open-eyed trance, and Blake marveled over the detail of the creation. Confident he understood what was going on; he sauntered up to the yeti. Leaning in, he examined the realness of its body. The fur looked like real fur. The face seemed to have real dimension, real form. The shiny, dark skin even had pores. The collarbones could be seen just under the taut chest skin. The huge feet and hands had well-defined joints. Rough, darkened nails protruded from its long fingers. Moving closer and bending over the mandala, Blake picked up a whiff of an unpleasant scent. The smell grew more intense as he identified the pungent odors of excrement and sweat. He pulled back. *How could the smell be created? The thing looks real, and now it even stinks.*

Blake stood with hands on hips, shaking his head. Moments ago, he had felt he had resolved the issue of what the creature was. He wasn't so sure now. Illusions didn't smell. Right or wrong, he resolved to settle the issue for himself. What could it hurt?

He disassociated himself with a niggling feeling in his gut, strode to the edge of the mandala, and thrust his hand toward the face of the yeti. With a quick jab, Blake felt the warmth and soft texture of its flesh.

In an instant, the creature's dark eyes turned to Blake and its brow ruffled. Its huge jaw dropped, revealing massive canines. It let out a blood-curdling scream, and Blake ran and collided with a wall. Stunned, he sank to his knees. He struggled to get up. Jerked from his meditation, the monk rose suddenly. The beast's screams continued unabated as Blake clung to the wall in fear, knowing he should get out. His feet would not move.

Mih teh leaped from the mandala and fled the cave. The butter lamps flared up as the entity rocked the atmosphere. The monk threw his arms into the air and then hurried to Blake. Taking hold of him by the shoulders, the man gazed at him inquisitively. He took a white ceremonial cloth from inside his monk's robe and dabbed it at Blake's forehead. Crimson spots dotted the cloth, and the monk pushed Blake's hand up to hold it in place.

"Who are you? What are you doing here?" the monk asked.

"My friend is stranded a few miles from here, and I came to get his equipment. I heard chanting, so I followed it to you."

The monk nodded. "This is serious, but so is the life of a man. Do you require assistance?"

Blake pulled the cloth from his head. The quantity of blood soaking the white material made him queasy. Finding a clean patch of white, he patted it to his wound and found comfort when it remained clean. "I think we'll be okay. I have the gear. I just need to get back to him."

The monk bowed. "As you wish. I must find the yidam and get him under control."

"Yidam?" Blake called after the monk who already pursued mih teh.

Chapter Twenty-Six

Blake dropped the bloodied cloth and staggered from the chamber. Back out on the ledge, darkness engulfed the valley. Returning for Ang was not an option. Blake would have to spend the night alone in the caves with the creature out there. Sighing deeply, he ran his hand over his forehead, pulling hair from the sticky, coagulated blood of his wound. He clicked his light on and ran it along the ledge. Uneasy with the yidam loose, he scanned the cave face. Nothing moved in the silence. Maybe he would be safe.

Although the ledge hadn't previously caused any concern, Blake proceeded with caution, resting a hand along the sandstone wall. The blow to his head stung as he lowered himself over the ledge, placing his boot in one of the toeholds. He felt he was moving in slow motion, keenly aware of each muscle. He eased himself down to the cave where his gear awaited him. Needing reassurance, he shone the light again out into the valley. Still nothing. He hesitated at the entrance to the cave, sweeping the light into the dark recess. Empty. His heavy hiking boots seemed to drain the last bit of energy from him, and he shuffled to the farthest corner of the cave and collapsed.

The monk had called it a yidam. What the hell was a yidam? Why would a monk meditate and bring forth such a monster? More than anything, he wished that Ang was with him. Ang would be able to tell him what this all meant. Alone in a cave with a creature on the loose, how could he expect to sleep? How dangerous was this conjured mih teh? Would the monk be able to catch and control it? Blake's heart pounded as his mind raced. He imagined the beast bursting into the cave and grasping him by the throat, lifting him off the ground. Blake searched the cave, looking for a weapon. He could hit the yeti with some of the climbing gear. If he could get the rope around its neck, maybe he could strangle it. Fire! Animals are afraid of fire. He had matches and a lighter.

Blake dug through the pack and retrieved a sweatshirt. He balled it up and wrapped it with twine. *Now, if yeti comes, I'll keep him back with flames.* He set that aside, pulled a small pocketknife from the backpack, and slid that into his pocket. Momentarily, all the planning calmed him, and he sat back down. He nervously picked at the remnants of black nail polish near his cuticles. Then he turned his ankh pendant over and over, growing more agitated.

His mind drifted back to mih teh. The huge creature had massive arms and powerful legs. It dwarfed Blake, and he realized a pocketknife and a fireball were inadequate weapons. His breathing grew shallow as panic rose. He glanced at the paltry sweatshirt and he saw that the matches and lighter were still in the pack. If the yeti appeared, he wouldn't be ready. Jumping up, he spilled the pack's contents onto the cave floor, searching for the lighter and matches, all the time growing more and more frantic. He had to find them. That thing could kill him. Cold sweat broke along his brow and he began to hyper-ventilate. He searched through the contents once and was about to go through it again when he heard a scraping sound behind him.

He spun around to face the intruder. Thrusting his hand into his pocket, he grasped the knife. A translucent being floated inches off the ground before him. It wasn't mih teh.

"Blake."

The familiar voice comforted him immediately. The Rinpoche radiated intense light that filled the whole cave. His wise and caring eyes soothed Blake, and with that his breathing came back under control.

"The yidam is loose!" Blake yelled.

The Rinpoche answered him, communicating telepathically. "I know this. It has occurred before and it will soon be remedied. Your mind runs free and without control, causing you distress. You are in no danger. Rest now. I must go to Ang."

Like an electric light being clicked off, the form of the Rinpoche disappeared. A halo of bright light illuminated the doorway around the cave entrance, leaving the rest of the cave in darkness. Blake felt a soothing warmness in his chest. His panic had evaporated, and he was left in peace. Even when he tried to force thoughts about Ang alone on the ledge, his mind couldn't hold onto them. An overpowering urge to sleep enveloped him, and he lay down on the hard cave floor.

Hunger stirred him from his sleep the next morning. As he stretched, he wondered about the appearance of the Rinpoche the night before. Was it real? Again, the question of reality swirled around him. His whole journey with Ang seemed to be centered around trying to pick and choose what was real and what was not. Would he ever have a handle on that?

Blake turned over and quickly pulled himself up. The cave's entranceway still sparkled with radiant light. He approached the light, trying to fight the stiffness that accompanies a night on a hard floor. The light seemed to hover as a thick yellow beam just at the edge of the stone surfaces. He reached a hand forward and poked his finger through it. Sparks of rainbow-colored light fizzled from the new opening. When he removed his finger, the light mended itself, filling in the hole and returning to yellow. His finger felt warm.

When he looked beyond the arc of light, he saw that the valley still sat in shadow. The sun had just begun to rise in the east. *Ang! I must get to Ang.*

Blake gathered his belongings and exited the cave. Looking behind him, he saw the entranceway had grown dark. He rushed out into the eerily gray morning, determined to get back to Ang as quickly as possible. *Will Ang know about the yidam? Will he have a story about encountering the Rinpoche?*

Blake jogged back to the rope bridge and crossed with the agility of a mountain goat. Putting his feet into the same tracks he had made through the snow the day before, he forced himself onward. At the sheer drop-off, he stayed against the wall and proceeded on without hesitation. He dismissed thoughts of wild animals and passed the mani stone. Blake climbed higher and higher, and the sun began to warm his back. Rounding the side of the mountain, he could see that the snow had not fallen in the area where he had left Ang. He made quick progress on the clear trail.

As he neared the ledge, he called out, "Ang! Ang! I'm coming."

No answer. Blake rushed to the ledge and screamed, "Ang! Ang!"

"Blake! Did you find it?" Ang answered.

"Thank God you're all right! Yeah, I found it."

Removing the nylon rope from the pack, Blake circled the boulder and secured the line. He got on his belly near the edge of the precipice and cast the line toward Ang.

"Here it comes!"

The rope bounced off the rock surface and fell toward Ang. Ang shuffled a few feet to catch it.

"Good. I have it," Ang shouted.

Blake watched while Ang tied himself with the rope and started to pull himself up. The Sherpa's strength and climbing ability clearly showed as he walked himself up the incline. From there, he kneeled and crawled to the top. Blake wound the slack rope as Ang advanced. Cresting the ridge, Ang threw his arms around Blake.

"Thank you," Ang said.

Blake fought back tears, "Sorry. It took so long."

"You did very well. You saved me."

The two sat together with their legs dangling over the ledge.

"Yesterday, I ran into snow high on the mountain. I was pinned down and lost so much time that I couldn't get back by nightfall."

Ang nodded. Clouds passed in front of the sun, casting them into shadow. "We better get moving. Another front could form. Early spring snows are very unpredictable."

Blake took the lead and Ang followed. An hour later they made their way over the rope bridge and into the valley of caves. Dark clouds approached from the east, bringing howling winds. The temperature dropped quickly, and they sought refuge in one of caves.

Shedding their gear, Ang said, "We made good time. You move like an experienced trekker now."

"Thanks. I guess I'm getting used to it."

They sat against the back wall of the cave, where they shared energy bars and downed some water. Ang turned on a camp light. Considerably colder than the night before, Blake put his gloves back on once he opened his food. There was much to talk about with Ang, but he hesitated, not knowing how to start.

The winds sliced through the canyon, echoing and moaning as if in pain.

Finally, Blake began. "I know this is going to sound weird. Did you see something last night? Like a ghost or a strange light?"

Ang sighed and crossed one leg over the other, straightening his back against the wall. "No, not that. I had a dream. The Rinpoche came to me and told me that you had made it to safety and that you would return in the morning."

"Did you think the dream was real?"

"I believed that you would come in the morning."

"It wasn't just the snow that kept me from making it back yesterday. I saw something, something I still can't explain."

Ang leaned forward. "Yes?"

Blake got up and went to the far corner of the cave. "When I was here yesterday, I heard chanting coming from a chamber above." He pointed to the ceiling. "So I went to investigate. Up there, a monk conjured a yidam inside an intricate sand design. At least, that's what he called it. It looked identical to the photos of mih teh."

Blake returned to Ang and their eyes met. Ang nodded.

"I touched it."

"You touched the yidam?" Ang said with concern.

"Right. It screamed and it wouldn't stop. Finally, it ran out of the room. Up until then, I thought it had been an illusion created by the monk somehow. But it was real, I felt it, I smelled it!"

"And the monk?"

Blake shrugged. "He took off after it."

"Ah," Ang said, crossing his arms over his chest. "That is why we had to come here."

Blake squatted. "What do you mean? I was supposed to see that...that thing?"

"I believe so. It is also why I am here. You are still struggling with reality and illusion. You believe that your mih teh is real because you touched it, smelled it."

"You bet your ass, it's real! It's as real as this." Blake picked up his water bottle and shook it.

"Quite so. We draw closer to the truth. You said this monk made this creature. Do you believe that to be so?"

"Looked like it to me."

"How can a man make a yeti? Did you see him gather flesh and bone and put it together?"

"No. No, of course not! It was some kind of magic."

"And you believe that magic creates reality?"

"You're confusing me again." Agitated, Blake pushed his hair out of his eyes and felt the rough scab that had formed over his injury from the day before. He began to pace.

"What is the source of this magic? Think!"

Blake shook his head. "I don't know what you want me to say. He chanted! It appeared!"

"Think of his tools. What did he use?"

Blake's pacing became more frantic. It was as if the whole journey rested on answering this one question correctly. *What did he use? What did he use?*

"His mind! He used his mind," Blake screamed.

Ang drew in a long breath and closed his eyes. "Yes."

Blake wrung his hands while he pondered the weight of this understanding. Yeti created from the mind, as real as his water bottle. That meant the water bottle could be a creation of the mind. No, the bottle had to be...he searched for the words...an illusion. Another creation of the mind.

Several moments passed before Blake said, "Is that what the Rinpoche wanted me to learn?"

"Perhaps this knowledge will allow you to consider the question of the photos in a new light."

Outside, the winds shifted and died. The sun broke through, chasing the chill from the valley. Blake and Ang met at the entrance of the cave and watched the transformation. Ang thumped Blake on the back and pulled him close. "Did you know the Karmapa, an important holy man, can control the weather?"

"Why not?" Blake said. He flashed a crooked smile at Ang.

"We will stay here tonight and head back tomorrow. It is time to go back to see the Rinpoche."

Ang extinguished the camp lamp and pulled out a small newspaper from his pack. The sun's warmth called to them. Ang sat with his legs overhanging the cave front. Lying in the entranceway, Blake propped himself up on both elbows and flipped open his Dante book, knowing he would never even glance down at it. The Rinpoche's question still remained unanswered. How would revealing the yeti photos affect the region?

First off, no one would accept that the yeti was a conjured being. Yidams didn't exist in the real world. And what did *real* mean anymore? Setting aside the fact that yeti was not what anyone ever expected, what would revealing the photos do? That question could be answered. Everyone would assume the creature was no longer myth but a living, breathing animal, previously unknown to science. Publication of the photos would bring media attention. This would soon draw scientists, tourists, and perhaps hunters. The home range for yeti could extend to several countries, not just Ang's native Nepal. Areas including Tibet, India, Bhutan, and China could all be affected. The tourist money might be a good thing. A modern economy could bring jobs, opportunity, prosperity, education and health care. Could tourism be a bad thing?

The Himalayan region might have to modernize to meet the needs of foreign tourists. Roads would need to be constructed and vehicles would need to be imported. New hotels, restaurants, and shops would be required. All this would lead to some measure of environmental impact. Unlike the infrastructure in place to support mountain climbing, a whole array of new services into very remote and isolated areas would develop. Villages that had lived in seclusion for hundreds of years might have to face a fast-moving, modern world. Would the people want that? Was that his decision to make?

In the couple of months Blake had been traveling, he had seen the way Buddhism permeated every aspect of life in the area. How would that be affected? Would villagers be drawn into the information age and cast off their religion and culture?

Could the monasteries retain their focus and keep alive their traditions, some of them secret?

Each question brought more questions to mind. Blake reeled with the knowledge that the mind created the yidam. That part, he was sure, the world was not ready for.

Accompanied by Ang, Blake traveled back through the countryside. With his body fully acclimated, he moved swiftly. He enjoyed revisiting the same sites and meeting up with friends he'd made along the way. At Thame, he watched with respect as the monks practiced tumo. Strolling through the market in Namche Bazaar, he smirked when he heard an American pop song spill from one of the shops. The reminder of home made him yearn for Katmandu to reconnect with Dad. Somehow, the anger he'd felt at the beginning of the journey had melted. He was anxious to see Dad now.

Surrounded by Himalayan peaks, Tengboche stood as a timeless gateway and guardian. The complex teemed with trekkers in shirtsleeves. Erected in front of the central monastery building, colorful modern tents looked like wildflowers in bloom. The affable mix of different languages and dress made the grounds bubble with excitement and energy.

"I can take you to see the Rinpoche," Ang said as they walked among the tents.

"No, you don't need to. I can do this by myself."

"Quite so. I will find accommodations, then."

Blake jogged up the steep monastery steps leading to the hall where the Rinpoche greeted travelers. Cresting the top stair, he broke into a brisk walk. No longer did he feel winded or fight headaches. His body had found peace in the high altitude.

Outside the Rinpoche's chamber, a young monk at a desk scribbled notes. Blake cleared his throat and drew his attention. The monk uttered a few foreign phrases, and Blake realized communication would be difficult. Now he wished he had brought Ang. Blake pointed to the Rinpoche's door and then pretended to hold a camera to his eye, clicking the imaginary device. The monk smiled, nodded, and bowed. He retreated behind the massive chamber door leaving Blake alone in the hallway. Moments later he was ushered before the Rinpoche.

The high lama sat cross-legged on a raised dais. He was draped in a simple burgundy robe, with wooden prayer beads wrapped around his wrist. Kind brown eyes set in wrinkled skin peered at him.

"Blake," the Rinpoche said. "I see you have returned to us. No doubt you will want your property returned." The Rinpoche reached behind his back and brought forth the camera and photos. He held them out for Blake to take. "I return these items to you, no questions asked." A smile broke on the old man's face.

"You know I won't take them, don't you?"

"Yes."

"Did you always know?"

"Nothing was certain. But I am interested in knowing why you changed your mind."

Even in the gravity of the moment, Blake couldn't help but chuckle. "I changed my mind because my mind has changed."

The Rinpoche leaned back and laughed at the clever turn of phrase.

Blake continued. "In the end, I saw that releasing the photos of the yeti would have consequences beyond what I could predict. I can't be responsible for that. You keep them. You decide."

The Rinpoche nodded. Unwinding the beads from his arm, he held them out for Blake to take.

"Thank you."

The holy man clasped Blake's hands in his own, chanting. "A safe and happy return to your father."

Blake bounded down the steps, passing tourists and monks. Ang sat midway down the stairs.

"Let's go say goodbye to Mr. Taylor," Blake said pulling him to his feet.

"Did you see the Rinpoche? Did you get the camera?"

"I saw the Rinpoche. I don't want the camera."

"You are sure?"

Blake sighed. "It's about the only thing I've been sure of in a long time!"

Ang delivered Blake to Katmandu the first week in June. Negotiating the tight, crowded streets of the city was difficult. People were everywhere. Even cattle roamed the lanes. Taxis honked and music blared. The aroma of exotic food mixed with the smell of sweaty people. Modern buildings stood side by side with dilapidated huts. Blake and Ang turned a corner and approached a two-story hotel sorely in need of paint. Out front, a cow munched on blue poppies in a ceramic container. They stepped around the animal and Ang threw the door open.

The overpowering smell of curry made Blake's eyes water while they waited at the counter for the hotel manager to buzz Blake's dad. Slipping off their packs, Blake and Ang dropped into two rattan chairs near the door. Footsteps pounded the stairs, and Andrew McCormack rushed into the room.

"Hey, guys!" he called.

Blake rose slowly. Dad grabbed him and pulled him tight. Blake's arms went around him.

"You need a bath! Bad!" Dad said, rubbing Blake's hair, not letting go.

"Yeah, it's been a while."

Dad finally released Blake and shook hands with Ang. "It's so good to see you both again! Take a seat, I'll bet you're tired."

They sat while Dad went to talk briefly with the manager.

Returning to them, Dad pulled up a folding chair. "Ang, I just want to say how grateful I am to you for taking care of Blake. I knew I could trust you."

"You are welcome. He is a good kid," Ang said.

"Blake, I know you were upset with me when I sent you away with Ang. This is my chance to make it up to you."

The manager set a tray of sandwiches and a pitcher of iced tea before them.

"I've worked it out with your mom, and she's willing to let you stay another week so I can show you the sights here. Sound good?"

"Yeah, Dad, but don't you need to get back to your practice?"

"Nah, that can wait. And Ang, you're welcome to join us."

"Thank you, but I will need to return to my family."

"All right then. I have one other surprise. I've booked a trek for the two of us next year. It goes right through Ang's village, so we'll see him next year."

"Cool!" Blake said picking up one of the sandwiches and tearing into it. Ang poured the tea and Blake savored it. The rest of the afternoon, he told Dad about the places he'd seen and some of what he had experienced. Some things he wasn't ready to share, but perhaps in time, he and Dad would be close enough to talk about all of it.

About the Author

Ellis Nelson has worked as an Air Force officer, government contractor, and teacher. She has had an interest in Buddhism since childhood. Currently she lives in the Denver area with her husband.

Website: http://www.ellisnelson.com

Jupiter Gardens Press

Jupiter Gardens Press, a division of Jupiter Gardens LLC, publishes metaphysical fiction and nonfiction, as well as science fiction and fantasy. Jupiter Gardens Press invites you to explore the entire Jupiter Gardens, LLC family.

Jupiter Gardens, LLC – http://www.jupitergardens.com/
Jupiter Gardens Press – http://www.jupitergardenspress.com/

Thank you for buying and reading our books! Our authors appreciate your patronage.

Thank you for your purchase. Please use code "snows" for 10% off your next purchase of Jupiter Storm YA novels direct from Jupiter Gardens Press!

CPSIA information can be obtained at www.ICGtesting.com
Printed in the USA
BVOW05s1054230914

367978BV00001B/102/P